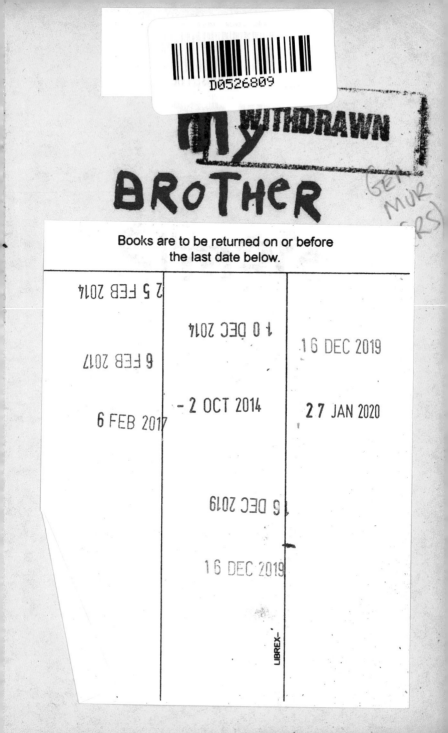

MY BROTHER

(GET
MUR
RS)

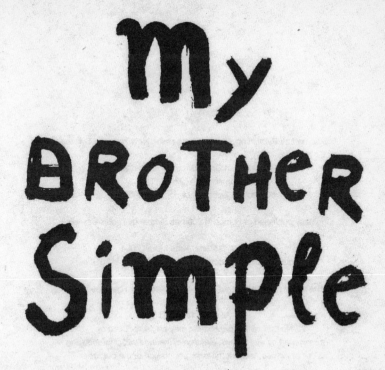

My Brother Simple

MARIE-AUDE MURAIL

Translated by Adriana Hunter

LONDON NEW DELHI NEW YORK SYDNEY

Bloomsbury Publishing, London, New Delhi, New York and Sydney

First published in Great Britain in August 2012 by
Bloomsbury Publishing Plc
50 Bedford Square, London, WC1B 3DP

Originally published in France in 2004 as *Simple* by *l'école des loisirs*

Copyright © Marie-Aude Murail 2004
English translation copyright © Adriana Hunter 2012

The moral rights of the author and translator have been asserted

A CIP catalogue record for this book is
available from the British Library

ISBN 978 1 4088 1471 0

MIX
Paper from
responsible sources
FSC® C018072

Typeset by Hewer Text UK Ltd, Edinburgh
Printed in Great Britain by Clays Ltd, St Ives Plc, Bungay, Suffolk

1 3 5 7 9 10 8 6 4 2

www.bloomsbury.com

With all my affection
To Christine Thiéblemont and her students,
'Too young for the grown-ups,
grown-up enough for life'
Jacques Higelin

Chapter 1

*Where Mister Babbit smashes
the phone*

Kleber gave his brother a sideways glance. Simple was imitating the sound the Métro doors made when they closed: '*Biiiing . . . clack.*'

A man got in at the station and sat down next to Kleber. He had a German shepherd dog on a lead.

Simple squirmed in his seat.

'He's got a dog,' he said.

The dog owner stared at him: what he saw was a young man with pale eyes filled with childish wonder.

'He's got a dog, the man has,' he said, getting more excited by the minute.

'Yes,' Kleber replied, trying to quieten him down with a frown.

'Do you think I can stroke it?' asked Simple, reaching his hand towards the dog.

'No!' Kleber snapped.

The man looked at the two brothers one after the other as if to evaluate the situation.

'I've got a bunny rabbit,' the young man with the pale eyes told him.

'You know you mustn't talk to strangers,' Kleber scolded.

Then he turned to the man with the dog.

'Look, I'm sorry. He's got learning difficulties.'

'An i-di-ot,' his brother corrected, articulating each syllable clearly.

The man got up without a word and tugged at the dog's lead. He got off at the next station.

'Prick,' grumbled Kleber.

'Uh-oh, bad word,' said his brother.

Kleber heaved a gloomy sigh and glanced at the window. He saw his own face reflected in it: not bad-looking, intellectual, with fine-rimmed round glasses. Recovering his composure, he settled back into his seat and looked at his watch. Simple, who was following his every move, pulled back the sleeve of his sweatshirt and examined his own wrist.

'I haven't got a watch.'

'You know exactly why you haven't. Shit, we're here!'

'Uh-oh, bad word.'

Kleber headed for the doors but turned back just as he was about to get out. Simple, who had initially followed him, had stopped.

'Hurry up!' called Kleber.

'They're going to get me!'

Kleber grabbed him by the sleeve and hauled him on to the platform. The automatic doors snapped closed behind them. *Clack.*

'They didn't get me!'

Kleber took his brother's sleeve again and dragged him towards the escalator.

'Why haven't I got a watch?'

'You broke it to see if there was a little man inside, remember?'

'Yeeeees,' said Simple with an ecstatic smile.

'Was there a little man inside?'

'No!' he roared, with the same enthusiasm.

He stopped so abruptly in front of the escalator that two people behind him telescoped into each other.

'Hey, watch what you're doing!' they protested.

Kleber tugged at his brother's sleeve once more to urge him on to the escalator. Simple looked down at his feet in terror, lifting them up off the steps. Then, reassured that they weren't doomed, he looked up.

'Did you see?' he asked once he was at the top. 'I wasn't even frightened. Why isn't there a lil'-man inside?'

'It's "little", not "lil",' Kleber corrected him, in an attempt to stop the stream of whys.

He heard his brother mutter, 'It's lil'man, lil'man.'

Simple's stubbornness was quite remarkable. For the next five minutes he chanted 'lilman, lilman' to himself.

Kleber looked around, not too sure which way they should go. They had only been in Paris a fortnight.

'Are we nearly there?'

'I don't know.'

Kleber was feeling stressed. He didn't recognise anything. Simple stopped in the middle of the pavement and crossed his arms.

'I want to see Daddy.'

'Daddy isn't here. He's in Marne-la-Vallée and we're, we're in . . . in . . .'

Simple blew a raspberry to finish his brother's sentence, then started laughing at his own brilliant joke. Kleber smiled weakly. Simple had a mental age of three, three and a half on a good day.

'We're in Paris. Come on, we need to hurry up. Otherwise it's going to get dark.'

'Will there be wolves?'

'Yes.'

'I can always shoot them with my vevolver, you know.'

Kleber stifled a snigger. They set off again and Kleber suddenly recognised the street. This was it. 45 Rue du Cardinal-Lemoine.

'Ohhhh no,' Simple said flatly when he saw the front door.

'What now?'

'Don't want to, it's that widold lady.'

'Look, she's our great-aunt, she's Mum's mum's –'

'She's ugly.'

'She's not very pretty.'

'She smells.'

Kleber's hand hovered over the entry-code panel, and he frowned in concentration.

'OK, it's 4 . . . 6 . . .'

'4, 6, B, 12, 1000, 100,' Simple rattled off briskly.

'Stop it. 4 . . . 6 . . .'

'9, 12, B, 4, 7, 12 . . .'

Kleber looked at the numbers, confused.

'Go on, push – push the buttons! 9, 7, 12 . . .'

Simple started punching the numbers randomly. The door buzzed and opened.

'I won!'

In fact, a very large woman was coming out. Simple barged past her to get in.

'You mustn't push past people like that!' Kleber cried. 'Say sorry to the lady.'

Simple had already gone up five stairs in two big strides. He turned round and chirped, 'Sorry, lady! You're too fat for the doorway!' and galloped on up the stairs. Kleber tried to catch up with him, yelling, 'It's on the third floor! The third floor!'

Simple climbed all six floors of the building, came back down four then up one again. He finally came to a stop on the landing, lolling his tongue and panting like a dog. Kleber leant against the wall for a moment, suddenly exhausted.

'Are you gonna press the button?' Simple said.

Simple was frightened of the sound the bell made. He blocked his ears as his brother rang it.

'Well, I've already had dinner,' muttered an old lady as she opened the door to them. 'We eat at six thirty, us old folks. Perhaps you young people don't eat at a set time, but I have my tea at six –'

'Nah, nah, nah.' Simple imitated her chattering stream of words.

'What's the matter with him?' said their great-aunt, raising her arms as if she was about to hit him.

'Leave him alone, he's not hurting anyone,' said Kleber.

'I'm gonna kill her, I am. I've got my vevolver!'

Simple took a toy gun from his pocket, and the old lady screamed.

'A gun!' she cried, 'a gun!'

'It's not real,' Kleber interjected.

'Yeah, but it's like it can really kill. You wait, when I say bang, you'll be dead. Watch out, widold lady . . .'

Simple slowly took aim at his great-aunt, who started shrieking in terror.

'Bang!'

The old woman fled towards the kitchen. Simple turned to his brother, both amazed and proud of the effect he had had on her.

'She's frightened.'

Then, disappointed all the same, added, 'She's not dead. I've got a knife, I have.'

'You can finish her off another time.'

After gobbling down a whole kilo of noodles between the two of them, they retreated to the tiny room that their great-aunt had given them. Kleber took out his mobile. Simple was still watching his every move.

'You've got a phone, you have,' he said enviously. 'Why haven't I got a phone?'

''Cos you're too young,' Kleber replied absent-mindedly. 'Now, 01 . . . 48 . . .'

'12, 3, B, 1000, 100.'

Kleber ran his hand over his forehead. His brother was distracting him again. Anyway, what good would it do calling their father? Mr Maluri thought there was only one solution: an institution. He would tell him to take Simple back to Malicroix.

'Hello-o!' said a mischievous voice.

Simple was sitting cross-legged on the bed, hiding something behind him. He said 'Hello-o!' again winningly. Two floppy, greyish fabric ears peeped out from behind his back. He waggled them.

'That's all we need,' mumbled Kleber.

'Who is it?'

'I don't know.'

He had to make the fun last.

'It begins with "ba",' said Simple.

'Is it a badger?'

'No!'

'Is it a baddy?'

Simple nearly collapsed laughing.

'Is it Mister Babbit?'

'Yeeeees!' Simple roared, brandishing an old toy rabbit. Its ears flopped about madly.

Kleber's mobile started ringing.

'My turn,' begged Simple. 'My turn. "Hello."'

Kleber leapt to his feet so his brother couldn't snatch the phone from him.

'Hello, Dad?'

'No, it's my turn, it's my turn. "Hello, Dad."'

'Yes, everything's fine,' Kleber said casually. 'We're here with Mister Babbit, everything's good . . . Auntie? She's fine too. Well, not really, actually.'

Kleber had made up his mind to tell his father.

'Simple doesn't really like her. He wants to kill her.'

Kleber didn't always think about what he was saying.

9

'No, no, not for real! With his vevolver . . . Yes . . .
yes . . . I dunno, Dad. He's my responsibility, I'm the
one who wanted . . . Yes.'

He raised his eyes to the ceiling while his father
justified his point: Simple was too much of a burden,
he made life impossible, he had to go back to Malicroix.

Meanwhile, Simple had emptied a whole bag of Playmobil toys on to the bed and was whispering to
himself as though absorbed in his game. But he was
keeping one ear on the phone conversation.

'He's naughty, that one.' Simple was talking about
a small black and white cowboy. 'He's going to the
intistution.'

Simple adopted an expression of grim satisfaction.
The little figure was subjected to threats, slaps and
an injection. Then he put him under his pillow.

'Help! help!' the little cowboy cried.

While he talked to his father, Kleber watched his
brother play.

'The best thing would be to find a room to rent. We'd
be independent . . . No, Dad, Simple doesn't need
"monitoring" the whole time. He's twenty-two.'

Simple had just taken the figure back out from under the pillow and was telling him off.

'You're an i-di-ot, I don't want to see your face again. I'm gonna dig a hole. You're gonna go in the hole and you'll be dead and I'm not gonna be sad about you, I'm not. Where's Mister Babbit gone?'

He scanned the bed frantically for his rabbit. When he saw him, he relaxed right away.

'Aaaah!' he said. 'There he is. Mister Babbit's going to kill Malicroix.'

Carnage ensued as Mister Babbit landed in the middle of the Playmobil pieces and began lobbing them in the air and hurling them against the wall.

'Mister Babbit's smashing the place up,' Simple said quietly to himself.

Then he glanced surreptitiously at his brother, who was still battling it out on the phone.

'Anyway we've got the money we inherited from Mum. You won't have to pay the rent . . . Yes, I know what I'm doing.'

Kleber switched off his mobile, having secured vague permission from his father. He stayed there for a while, staring vacantly and hugging the mobile to his chest. Seventeen. He was seventeen. He had just enrolled for the second year of sixth form at a local college. He had ambitions of going to a top university. And everywhere he went he took his freak of a brother with him, Simple, whose real name was Barnaby, who thought cuddly toy rabbits were alive.

'Simple?'

Simple stopped playing and said 'My brother!' as if God had just spoken to him.

'OK, now listen, Simple, we're going to find a place for us both to live. But I can't be with you all the time because in two weeks I have to go back to college.'

'That's not good, college isn't.'

'Yes it is.'

'So why don't I go, then?'

'I told you to listen. If you want to stay with me, you're going to have to make an effort.'

Simple listened, his mouth open, utterly willing.

'D'you understand. You've got to help me.'

Simple leapt to his feet.

'I'm gonna tidy all the bed.'

'That's right . . .' Kleber sighed.

*   *   *

First thing the following morning, Kleber decided to visit some letting agencies. He hesitated for a while before leaving Simple at home.

'Will you be good?'

Simple nodded so vigorously his head nearly came off.

'You won't annoy Auntie?'

Simple shook his head before adding a rather contradictory, 'I've got my knife, I have.'

On the doorstep Kleber was still feeling unsure about leaving Simple on his own. It would be better if there was a way to contact him, so he decided to entrust Simple with his mobile. Full of fear and amazement, Simple cradled it in both hands. Kleber explained that he would call him later in the morning to see what he was up to.

'OK, so when it rings, you press on the little green phone.'

Kleber set off with the picture of his brother paralysed with delight fresh in his mind. The moment the front door had swung shut, Simple bellowed, 'Mister Babbit!'

He blundered off into the bedroom, where the rabbit was snoozing on his pillow.

'What's all the shouting about?' Mister Babbit asked.

'I've got the phone!' Simple yelled.

Mister Babbit sat up. 'Give it here, then!'

'No, it's mine. 4, 7, 12, B, 1000, 100.'

He punched in some numbers, then put the phone to his ear.

'Hello?' he said. 'Hello, Mr Somebody?'

He seemed to listen for something, then shook the phone and put it back to his ear.

'Hello, Mr Somebody? . . . It's not working.'

Mister Babbit lay down again, his long limp arms behind his head, feigning indifference.

'It works when there's a lil'man inside.'

'There isn't a lil'man,' said Simple, remembering the drama with the watch.

'There is but he only comes when the phone rings.'

Simple looked at Mister Babbit for a long time, trying to think of an answer to that.

'OK,' he said, giving up on the phone, 'shall we play?'

On first examination, Mister Babbit could be taken for a very old rabbit, with fur rubbed bare in places. But as soon as there was any talk of playing, his ears quivered frenetically and his floppy legs seemed to spring to life.

'What are we playing?'

'The Malicroix game.'

'Again! Haven't you got another game?'

'But it's a good one.'

Simple leant towards Mister Babbit and whispered in his ear, 'You can smash people's faces in.'

At around ten o'clock, when the cowboy was surrounded by other figures to stop him escaping, the mobile started ringing.

'My turn, my turn!' Simple shouted.

Half crazed with excitement, he pressed the telephone symbol.

'Hello, Simple?' said Kleber.

'Hello, Mr Somebody? Hello, how are you? I'm very well, thank you, it's a lovely day, goodbye.'

'Wait, it's me, your brother . . .'

A little afraid, Simple turned to Mister Babbit, 'It's the lil'man.'

'Smash the phone!' Mister Babbit ordered, leaping about on the spot. 'Smash it on the wall!'

Simple threw the phone against the wall with a sort of terrified violence. Then he finished the job by stamping on it with his heel. When he had calmed down, he leant over and peered at the shattered mobile.

'Can you see him?' Mister Babbit enquired, ready to make a run for it.

'N-n-nooo,' Simple said cautiously.

'I knew it,' said Mister Babbit, lying back down on the pillow. 'He's titchy!'

After his abortive phone call, Kleber decided to go back to the Rue du Cardinal-Lemoine. He laughed as he remembered Simple running through his repertoire of grown-up niceties. Kleber felt like being happy. The girl at the agency was definitely into him. She'd promised to show him round a one-bedroom apartment that afternoon. Kleber felt he was quite capable of getting the girl and the apartment.

'Simple! Simple?'

He found his brother sitting on the bed, fiddling with the cowboy.

'Were you frightened? What's the matter?'

He caught sight of the phone spewing its guts out on the floor by the wall.

'There's no lil'man,' Simple said desolately.

* * *

16

The appointment was set for two o'clock. Kleber didn't want to leave Simple alone at home. As he was only seventeen himself, the fact that his brother was twenty-two had reassured the girl at the lettings agency. It all came down to whether Simple could maintain the illusion for the length of their visit.

'You've got to be good. Don't say anything. Don't run all over the place.'

Simple greeted each of his brother's sentences with a silent nod. Kleber had been really hard on him about the phone.

'Brush your hair. Wash your hands. And . . . I'm going to put a tie on you.'

Simple's moping face lit up. Half an hour later he was admiring himself in the mirror in the hall. He had a shirt and tie on, a light-coloured jacket and dark trousers. Kleber didn't look quite so impressed. On Simple's body even the most beautifully cut clothes ended up looking like something that a scarecrow might wear.

'Remember – don't say a word!'

Kleber put his finger over Simple's mouth to reinforce the instruction. Of course he could try and pass him off as a deaf mute but it would be risky. Simple was quite capable of *explaining* that he was a mute to the girl from the agency.

The little apartment was at the top of an old building on the Avenue du Général-Leclerc. Isabelle was waiting for her clients upstairs. She had substituted chewing gum for cigarettes two months earlier, but had recently given in and was now smoking and chewing gum at the same time. She was thinking about Kleber. Not bad-looking. And he had an older brother. If he was anything like Kleber, this could be interesting. Isabelle bit her nails as she smoked and chewed her gum.

At the bottom of the stairs Kleber was finishing briefing his brother.

'Don't say a thing and don't move. You haven't brought your vevolver, I hope?'

'No.'

Kleber climbed up two stairs.

'But I have got my knife,' Simple said behind him.

Kleber turned round. 'What is all this about a knife? Where is this knife of yours?'

Simple blinked but said nothing.

'Are you going to show it to me?'

'No,' said Simple with an embarrassed laugh.

'I'll get angry! Do you want me to get angry?'

Sometimes Kleber lost it. Simple's eyes filled with panic.

'It's not a real knife.'

'Show me.'

'Smywiwi.'

'What?'

Simple climbed on to the stair below Kleber and stood on tiptoe to whisper in his ear.

'It's my willy.'

For a minute Kleber couldn't believe what he was hearing.

'Don't be an arsehole.'

'Uh-oh, bad word,' said Simple.

Now they were late and had to race up the six flights of stairs.

Isabelle was amazed when she saw the two brothers come in. They were alike but the younger one looked older. He had brooding eyes fed by some internal fire, while the other one had eyes so clear they looked like windows open to the sky. You almost expected to see swallows flitting across them. Kleber had short hair, in keeping with the note of controlled seduction in his smile. Simple had long, tangled, straw-coloured hair, and didn't seem to be quite there. Isabelle held out her hand to him.

'Good afternoon,' she managed to say.

Already forgetting all his promises, Simple started reciting, 'Good afternoon, how are you? Thank you, goodb—'

'So, this is the living room!' Kleber cried, trying to smother his brother's words.

Isabelle was startled.

'Yes, the living room,' she said. 'It's very light as you can see. It faces south-west.'

Simple stood there fidgeting in front of her. She couldn't help staring at him.

'I've got a tie on,' he said, not sure the lady had noticed.

She gave a brief half-smile, more of a facial twitch than an expression.

'Well, nowadays, you do have to make a good impression to find somewhere to live.'

She felt so awkward she took another cigarette from her packet and snapped on the flame of her lighter.

'That's dangerous,' said Simple, who had been told never to play with fire.

'Yes, I'm going to give up,' Isabelle replied, irritated.

'And is there another room?' Kleber went on.

'Oh, yes, a north-facing room. It's not as bright but it overlooks the courtyard so it's quieter . . .'

Kleber and Isabelle went through to the other room. Simple didn't follow them. He looked around, open-mouthed. His brother had told him they were going to live here . . . but there weren't any chairs, or a table, anything! Simple tiptoed forward, afraid of waking some magic power in this mysterious place. Then he noticed a door standing ajar. He opened it and found a cupboard set into the wall. Empty. Simple smiled, put his hand in his pocket and took out two Playmobil characters. He had brought a whole collection of bits and bobs with him. He arranged them on the shelves, creating a miniature version of an apartment. Forgetting where he actually was, he talked quietly to himself as he played with his head in the cupboard. Isabelle came back into the sitting room with Kleber.

'Are you looking at the cupboards?' she asked

Simple. 'That's a real plus point in this apartment. Lots of built-in storage space.'

She opened the door wide.

'Oh, one of the last tenant's children has left some toys. I'm sorry . . .'

She reached out her hand to clear away the Playmobil figures.

'My Playmos!' howled Simple, turning to his brother in outrage. 'She's stealing my Playmos! I'll kill her, I will. I've got my knife!'

Terrified, Isabelle dropped the figures and backed towards the bedroom.

'Stop it, Simple!' cried Kleber. 'Don't worry, he's got learning difficulties. He's . . .'

Simple rammed his toys back into his pocket.

'Get out of here! Go on, get out!' Isabelle ordered.

'All right, there's no need to talk to us like that,' said Kleber. 'Anyway, it's way too expensive for what it is, with only one bedroom. Come on, Simple. We don't want this place.'

Simple threw a triumphant scowl at the girl from the agency.

'There isn't any chairs or anything!'

*   *   *

Back outside, Kleber made no comment. As the day wore on he felt he was slipping into an increasingly weird world. He was beginning to act like an automaton. He held his brother back on the edge of the pavement when he was about to launch out in front of the traffic.

'The lil'man's red,' he told him.

When they got to the other side, Simple rapped on the glass over the lil'man, who was now green. Deep down, Kleber felt sorry for him. If he couldn't find somewhere for them to live, he would have to take Simple back to the care home at Malicroix.

On the way home Kleber noticed a rusting metal plaque outside the Vieux Cardinal Hotel: *Rooms to let by the week*. He thought they could always rent a room until they found an apartment. They had to get away from their great-aunt.

'Come on,' he said, tugging Simple by the sleeve.

The hall was deserted and smelled of dust. There were a few keys hanging behind the counter, looking as if they had been waiting for customers a long time.

'Hello?' Kleber called.

Simple thrust his hands anxiously into his pockets.

A girl with heavy make-up and a short skirt came

23

over to the Maluri brothers. Simple loved it when women wore 'pretty-smell'. He gave her a beaming smile.

'Well, how are *you*?' she asked him, taking hold of his tie.

Kleber watched her, rooted to the spot.

'I've got a tie on,' said Simple, terribly proud that the lady had noticed straight away.

'And what am I going to do with you, my bunny rabbit?' she asked him, half closing her eyes.

Hearing the word 'bunny', Simple reached gently for something in his pocket.

'Hello-o,' he said mischievously.

Two floppy ears wriggled from his pocket.

'What's that?' the girl asked cautiously.

'*Who* is that?' Simple corrected. 'It's my little friend. It ends in "it".'

Shit, Kleber thought and took his brother by the sleeve.

'Come on,' he muttered.

Simple pulled his rabbit out by the ears and waggled it in the girl's face. She gave a terrified shriek.

'It's Mister Babbit!' bellowed Simple.

As Kleber dragged his brother out on to the street, he heard the girl shout, 'They're sick, the pair of them!'

Kleber was in no hurry to get back to their great-aunt's gloomy apartment. He decided to show Simple the magnificent honeyed white stone building of Henri IV college.

'You see that, that's my college.'

'Yuck.'

They continued their stroll till they reached the Jardin du Luxembourg. Simple wanted to show Mister Babbit the little sailing boats on the pond. The Maluri brothers sat down beside the pond, and Simple put the rabbit on his lap.

'You're wrecking your Babbit,' Kleber pointed out. 'You mustn't squash him into your pocket like that.'

'It's not Babbit, it's Mister Babbit.'

'OK,' Kleber murmured with a smile.

He watched some children running round the pond to catch up with their boats. He dipped his fingers in the water and made a small splashing sound. The sun was going down. He didn't give a toss about what other people might think of Simple and his rabbit. He took his hand back out of the water and put it on Simple's knee.

'Shall we go?'

'You've got me wet with water.'

Before going home, they stopped at the local mini-market for a chocolate bar. Waiting at the till, Kleber read the small ads pinned up by other customers. Fate was giving him a sign: *Two rooms available in student flatshare.* Kleber made a note of the number on a used Métro ticket.

Back at their great-aunt's apartment, Simple said he wanted a bath. He started by taking a bag of Play-mobil to the bathroom.

'Don't put Mister Babbit in the water,' Kleber warned.

'No.'

'Leave him on your bed.'

'Yes.'

The moment his brother had his back turned, Simple wrapped Mister Babbit in his pyjamas and snuck off to the bathroom.

'Hey, you're suffocating me!' whinged Mister Babbit, freeing himself. He sat on the washing machine and watched the bath filling up. 'Are you putting bubble bath in?'

Simple opened the blue bottle and emptied a good quarter of its content into the water.

'More! More!' cried Mister Babbit, hopping from one leg to the other.

'That's naughty,' Simple told him sternly.

Mister Babbit pretended he hadn't heard.

'Shall we make a campsite?

Simple had a Playmobil tent and some skiers and a boat and some penguins. Together they made a seriously convincing campsite.

'I've lost a ski,' said Simple.

He tipped the whole bag on to the tiled floor and started searching.

'Shit,' said Mister Babbit.

'Uh-oh, bad word.'

'Who cares?'

They sniggered. Then both of them dived into the bubbles, drowned a few skiers, saved a few penguins and rowed between some icebergs. An hour later the bath was cold, the floor flooded and Mister Babbit heavy with water.

'I weigh a ton,' he said.

'Shit,' Simple concluded.

Kleber had to be alerted to the disaster.

'What a mess! And you've got your rabbit soaked again. You can clear the whole lot up for me.'

Simple didn't wait to be told again. All the Playmobil pieces disappeared into the bag.

'I've lost a ski.'

'Tragic,' said Kleber.

He wrung out the soft toy as best he could and hung it from the washing line by its ears.

'You'll be the death of this poor rabbit.'

Simple looked at Mister Babbit and shrugged. Kleber studied the toy for a while. One day it would fall apart. The thought made him heavy-hearted.

Chapter 2

Where Mister Babbit finds a burrow
but it's not great

Enzo was not into being woken at seven o'clock in the morning by Aria and her boyfriend. Hearing them having sex in the next room reminded him of his condition as a male of the species without a female. Enzo was twenty-one, fair-haired and not bad-looking, and he could, if he took the trouble, have found himself a girlfriend. But he wanted girls to tumble into his arms without actually having to tumble them. He hadn't yet worked out whether this was out of laziness or pride.

'Any coffee left?' Corentin asked, coming into the kitchen.

'Mm . . .'

Too early to get any words out.

'Someone rang yesterday about the flatshare,' Corentin went on. 'For him and his brother.'

'More blokes,' Enzo sighed.

Four people lived at 99 Rue du Cardinal-Lemoine: Enzo, Aria and her boyfriend Emmanuel, and Corentin, Aria's brother.

'Why can't we find any girls to share?' Enzo whined.

'Well, start looking!'

Corentin poured himself a coffee.

'This guy seemed OK. He's twenty-two and his brother's seventeen.'

On the phone, Kleber had passed himself off as the older of the two.

'Hey, hang on, it doesn't say kindergarten over the door!' Enzo snapped, then added half-heartedly, 'What's he studying?'

Corentin tried to get his memory in gear.

'I can't really remember. His brother's in his last year at Henri IV.'

'Sixth-formers are so boring,' grumbled Enzo. 'Going on about the difference between reggae and ragga, moaning about girlfriends, and smoking shit. Can't stand them.'

'Pass us the Nutella, Grandpa.'

'See? You're young. Nutella's a young thing. I like honey on my bread.'

'Ah bless, like Winnie the Pooh.'

'Do you think girls go for Winnie the Pooh? The best I'll get is Tigger. Pass the Nutella back.' Enzo delved his spoon into the pot glumly, and said, 'I always thought he was gay.'

'Winnie the Pooh?'

'No!' Enzo retorted indignantly. 'Tigger.'

'Oi, stop eating that straight from the pot. It's disgusting.'

'No, it's young.'

Corentin sighed. You couldn't get much out of Enzo on mornings like this.

'Morning, boys!'

It was Aria, cheeks still rosy from being in bed with Emmanuel, her short hair a mess of tufts, and looking so sexy in her scantily buttoned pyjamas that it hurt. She gave her brother a good morning kiss, patted Enzo on the head and took a huge bite out of a piece of stale bread. She was mesmerising, and had no inkling of the effect she had. Enzo and Corentin watched her, open-mouthed.

'What time are they coming to see the flat?' she asked, sitting down with one leg folded beneath her.

'Hey, hang on, I'm not necessarily going to like them!' said Enzo.

'More likely they won't like the rooms,' Aria parried.

The four of them had given themselves the best rooms. The two remaining rooms were small, cold and awkward-shaped.

Emmanuel came into the kitchen. At twenty-five he was the eldest.

'Heeeere's Tigger,' Enzo greeted him.

Aria's boyfriend looked at Enzo with a wary smile.

'Why Tigger?'

Corentin started laughing.

'Because I'm Winnie the Pooh,' Enzo replied, stretching. 'And Corentin's Rabbit.'

'Still just as much of a prick,' grumbled Emmanuel.

'Mind you, you'd be just as convincing as Eeyore,' Enzo went on, then imitated the donkey's depressive voice, 'Good morning, if you can call it a good morning . . .'

Emmanuel glanced at Aria, bewildered. To think this loser was doing a degree in literature! As punishment, Aria rapped Enzo on the head again, and he retaliated by digging his fingers into her groin. Aria let out a squeal and began pummelling Enzo with her fists. Emmanuel just stood there at first, unsure what to do.

'OK, guys! I think it's time to calm down now!'

Enzo leapt to his feet and offered his chair to Emmanuel.

'Please sit down, it's still warm.'

They gave each other a confrontational stare. Emmanuel sensed a rival in Enzo but not a serious one.

After breakfast, they each started their day's activities. Enzo went back to lie on his bed.

'Is this a good time?'

Corentin had just come into his room.

'What do you think?' Enzo replied, leaning on one elbow.

'What are you up to?'

'Nothing.'

Corentin sat down. Enzo had been his role model since Year 7.

'They're coming for coffee.'

'Who?' Enzo asked, his voice barely audible. He had dropped back down on to his bed as if he could no longer bear the weight of the world.

33

'The flatmates, of course. Well, the potential flatmates. You need to see them.'

In Corentin's eyes, if Enzo said yes, then the brothers would be in. If he said no, they would be rejected.

'Don't give a rat's arse,' Enzo muttered, his eyes closed.

'What's the matter?'

Corentin was not great at deciphering the human heart, but he could tell something was up with his friend.

'I . . .'

Enzo suddenly sat up and thumped the wall.

'I don't like being woken at seven in the morning by your sister and that other corpse-dissector, that's what's the matter!'

Emmanuel was studying medecine. Aria was too. Enzo lay down again, annoyed at having given himself away.

'Are you in love?' Corentin asked eventually.

'You what? No way! It's just a question of . . . decency. They should think about the fact that I'm just through the wall.'

Corentin didn't press the point. He looked up to his elder sister and was pretty intimidated by Emmanuel,

34

who was tall and well-built, and serious. He stood up with a sigh.

'Will you be here at lunchtime?'

'Where else would I be?'

Nope, definitely not a day to get anything out of Enzo.

Meanwhile, Kleber had been stressing out all morning.

How was he going to introduce his brother? Would he let him speak?

'Have you washed your hands?'

For the tenth time Simple turned on the taps. His brother's nerves were panicking him.

'Right. You're not taking your vevolver, OK?'

'I've got my knife.'

Kleber gave him an even more steely stare than usual.

'Ha hie hay hi-her ha-hi,' Simple mumbled.

'What?'

Simple stood on tiptoes and whispered in his brother's ear.

'Can I take Mister Rabbit?'

He was begging. Kleber wavered. Then, remembering

the effect the rabbit's appearance usually had, said firmly, 'Leave him here.'

But, just as they were leaving, Kleber went to look for his new mobile and Simple took the opportunity to stuff Mister Babbit into his pocket.

'Why haven't I got a phone?' he asked, all innocently.

'Because you broke mine.'

'Why did I break your phone?'

'Because you're a prick.'

'Uh-oh –'

'Yes, I know, bad word!'

Kleber was almost hysterical with nerves.

The apartment was just two blocks away.

'My turn to press the button, my turn!' cried Simple when he saw the entry-phone.

His brother grabbed him by the collar of his jacket.

'Right, listen to me. Either you behave yourself or I'll send you back to Malicroix.'

Simple's face drained of colour, and Kleber was instantly filled with remorse. He pressed on the button simply labelled 'FLATSHARE'.

'Yes?' said a girl's voice.

'Barnaby and Kleber Maluri.'

The building's hallway was quite grand. The curtain to the concierge's little apartment twitched, and she stared at the two brothers. Kleber decided against the old lift with its wrought-iron grille, and took the stairs. Simple was impressed by the red carpeting, and went up on tiptoes as if afraid of stepping on eggshells.

'Were you afraid of the lift?' Aria asked, letting them in. 'Hi . . . Are you Barnaby?'

She was speaking to Kleber. The teenager was a foot taller than his brother so she took him to be the older of the two.

'No, I'm Kleber.'

'Oh, sorry. I mean, sorry.'

The two brothers were now in the apartment, and Aria offered Simple her hand, saying, 'So, by deduction, you must be Barnaby. I'm Aria.'

There was an awkward pause because Simple shook her hand without saying anything.

'And . . . um . . . the others are in the living room, having coffee,' Aria added. 'Come on in.'

Emmanuel was reading, Corentin smoking, Enzo doing nothing. The coffee cups were waiting on the table alongside a plate of shortbread biscuits. There was a ripple of hellos when the Maluri brothers came into the room. Everyone sat round the table, and Emmanuel took charge of the interview.

'So, you're looking for somewhere to live?'

Kleber explained their temporary accommodation with an elderly relative, and how they wanted to be independent.

'What are you studying?' Emmanuel asked, making the same mistake as Aria.

'I'm just going into upper sixth.'

All eyes turned to Simple. He had his hands under the table and his eyes lowered.

'Right, OK,' said Kleber. 'This is my older brother. He's re— He has learning difficulties.'

In the ensuing silence Kleber felt out of his depth.

'Yes, I suppose that . . . that it would be a problem for you,' he said quietly.

Aria felt uncomfortable for him.

'Is he a mute?'

'God no! No, he's just intimidated at the moment.'

Simple was sneaking little upward glances, which didn't create a brilliant impression.

'Do you want to say something, Simple?' his brother whispered.

The young man shook his head very timidly.

'Has he been like this since birth?' Emmanuel asked.

'Yes. They think that . . . Well, it was probably something that happened during the pregnancy.'

'A sort of autism?' Emmanuel ploughed on.

'Come on! This isn't a consultation!' Enzo protested, turning to Kleber to add, 'Right, this isn't going to work. We're students. We could have taken you, no problem, but your brother . . . he can't be left to his own devices. He should be in a . . . some sort of specialised place.'

Aria glowered at him, outraged.

'Look, I'm a nice guy too!' Enzo struck back. 'It's just this sort of thing's beyond us. We can't be responsible . . .'

'It all depends on his particular condition,' said Emmanuel. Whatever Enzo said, Emmanuel always had to disagree with him. 'Is he having treatment?' he asked Kleber. 'Does he go to an outpatients clinic?'

Just then, Simple grunted.

'Ha hie haha hihi.'

'Ah, there you are! He can make noises,' said Enzo.

Simple spoke to Aria and Aria alone.

'Can I have a biscuit?'

'Yes, here . . .' She handed him a biscuit in the tips of her fingers as if giving it to a little dog. Kleber had never felt so humiliated. He made one last attempt.

'He actually has the IQ of a three-year-old.'

'Really? Just like Corentin,' said Enzo, who never missed an opportunity to wind up his friend.

His joke eased the tension. Aria poured the coffee.

'Can he have some?' she asked Kleber.

''Course not, it'll make him too hyper,' Emmanuel intervened.

Kleber was gobsmacked by how stupid they all were. Worse than their great-aunt! But the more Kleber suffered, the bolder his brother grew. The biscuit and Aria's smile probably had something to do with it.

'She's a very pretty lady,' he said, apparently speaking mainly to his shortbread.

'In fact, he's more advanced than Corentin,' Enzo remarked.

Simple stared at him and, pointing him out shyly to his brother, whispered, 'What's his name?'

'My name's Winnie the Pooh,' Enzo announced. 'And this,' he pointed to Corentin, 'is Rabbit.'

Hearing the word 'rabbit', Simple shot his hand into his pocket and there were soon two ears peeping above the table.

'Hello-o,' said Simple, waggling the ears.

'What the hell's that?' asked Enzo, looking disgusted.

'Who's that?' Simple corrected with a note of triumph. 'His name begins with "ba".'

'It's Mister Babbit,' said Kleber, eager to get this over with.

'Yeeeees!'

Simple brandished the rabbit by the ears. Emmanuel recoiled into the depths of his chair.

'Whoa! Doesn't he have to take pills when he gets like this?'

Seeing that Emmanuel was worried, Enzo took the opposite side.

'Hey, hang on, I think the dude's a laugh! And he's got a cool rabbit.'

'I've got a knife,' said Simple.

'And I've got a bayonet!' said Enzo in a childish voice.

Simple started laughing as if he understood the joke.

'He seems good-natured,' Corentin chipped in. He was offering support, sensing that Enzo was changing his mind.

'He's very affectionate,' Kleber confirmed, suddenly finding renewed hope. He was also thinking there would be plenty of time to talk about phones, the vevolver and all the other little details that gave life with his brother its own special charm. Aria poured Simple some coffee, and he slurped it down, pulling a variety of faces.

'Would you like to see the rooms?' she offered.

Kleber couldn't believe his ears. They might just be accepted.

The two free rooms were at the end of the corridor. They had only basic furniture and skanky wallpaper. Kleber was in heaven: the rooms had a connecting door.

When he realised that one of these rooms was intended for him, Simple announced, 'It's yuck.'

Aria, who had shown them the way, agreed. 'We kept the nicest rooms for ourselves, very selfishly.'

'It doesn't matter at all. We'll be absolutely fine.'

Kleber was happy and it showed. Aria, who really did lead a pretty selfish life, was pleased. She was doing a favour to a nice guy and his handicapped brother.

'So,' she said brightly, 'when are you moving in?'

There were some administrative details to sort out, and the conversation was likely to prove boring for Simple.

'I've brought some toys for you,' Kleber told his brother, opening his backpack and taking out some Playmobil figures.

'Have you got the vevolver?'

'No, I didn't bring it.'

'No, I mean the Playmo one for the cowboy,' Simple insisted.

Aria watched the brothers, slightly alarmed despite her best intentions.

'Um . . . I'll wait for you in the living room,' she said.

The moment she had gone, Kleber snatched his brother by his jacket.

'OK, you, now listen . . .'

'I don't want to go to Malicroix,' Simple begged.

'No, no, you won't,' Kleber soothed, then whispered, 'They're letting us have the rooms. We're going to live here. But you've got to be good. Can I leave you on your own in your room to play?'

'I'm not on my own!' He waggled his rabbit. Kleber glanced round the room to check there were no alarm clocks or telephones, anything that could be suspected of housing a lil'man. Then he went back to the living room.

'It's great,' he said straight away.

He accepted the financial terms, the share of domestic chores and the communal rules. Then came the awkward questions.

'Who's going to take care of your brother when you're in lessons?' asked Emmanuel.

'He's used to being left on his own. He plays, does some colouring, looks at his picture books . . .'

'TV?' Corentin guessed.

'Not much. More DVDs of cartoons.'

'I've got the whole collection of Winnie the Pooh,' offered Enzo.

He was delighted they were going to have an idiot in the apartment.

*   *   *

While Kleber made every effort to charm the flatmates, Mister Babbit was taking possession of his new burrow.

'It's not great,' he said.

Then he noticed the duvet on the double bed.

'Can we make a cave?'

Not many people know that duvets make excellent rabbit caves. Simple hauled it off the bed and moulded it into shape, propping it with the pillows and a bolster. Mister Babbit ventured in, ears first.

'Is it any good?' asked Simple.

Mister Babbit went all the way in, and his muffled voice could be heard whinging, 'It's not great.'

He came back out, adding, 'There aren't even any chairs.'

'Yes, but it's quiet and faces north, south, south-west,' Simple recited, putting to good use his recent exposure to letting agencies.

'Haven't you got any chairs?' Mister Babbit insisted.

Simple looked around and smacked his forehead with his palm. Of course he had! There were some paperbacks on a shelf. Excellent rabbit furniture. All the books disappeared under the duvet, providing a table, chairs and a bed.

'The bed's hard!' grumbled Mister Babbit.

A folded doily became a mattress. With all that diving in and out of Mister Babbit's burrow, Simple grew very hot. He took off his jacket, then his shirt, shoes and socks.

'*I*'ve got nothing on at all,' Mister Babbit encouraged him. 'You'll just have to take everything off.'

Simple refused to because of the knife. After an hour of this game, the room was in the advanced stages of pandemonium, with toys and clothes strewn over the carpet, and a terrible mess at the end of the bed. Kleber came back to fetch his brother, escorted by Enzo.

'Simple, what the hell are you doing?'

Simple looked round rather guiltily.

'I'm making a shambles.'

Enzo peered in.

'He can certainly trash a place in record time.'

'He'll clear it up.'

After four o'clock, Kleber didn't have the energy to feel irritated any more.

'Clear all this up,' he told Simple. 'And why've you taken your clothes off?'

'To be a rabbit.'

*   *   *

The next few days were happy ones. The Maluri brothers busied themselves with moving house. To be more accurate, Kleber packed up their things while Simple gave Mister Babbit a running commentary of the preparations.

'This is the best day of my life,' he announced when Kleber found the second Playmobil ski under a piece of furniture.

If, at that precise moment, anyone had offered to give Kleber someone normal in exchange for his brother, he would have refused.

'Come on, let's go and say goodbye to our great-aunt.'

Kleber kissed the old lady and thanked her for her hospitality.

'Are you going to give Auntie a kiss, Simple?'

'No. She stinks.'

The two brothers made a rapid exit.

When they were by the entry-phone to the new apartment, Kleber let his brother press the 'FLAT-SHARE' button. But Simple couldn't restrict his enthusiasm to one button and pressed all the others, muttering, '7, 9, 12, B, 1000, 100.'

'Hello?'

'Yes?'

'Who is it?'

Simple looked suspiciously at the entry-phone.

'There's loads of lil'men inside.'

In the hallway the curtain twitched, and the concierge watched the new tenants walk past.

The four students had gathered in the living room to drink to the Maluri brothers' arrival. Kleber had had opportunities to chat with them during the move, but Simple had not yet set foot in the apartment again. Like the first time, he seemed intimidated. He had a backpack crammed with toys, and he was clinging on to it.

'Can he have a glass of wine?' Aria asked Kleber.

'Of course he can't,' said Emmanuel, 'it'll interact with his medication.'

The future doctor was still convinced that Simple was stuffed full of tranquillisers. He turned to Kleber. 'Was an area of his brain damaged during the birth?'

'Emmanuel, you're very thoughtful,' Enzo intervened, 'but you can wait till people are dead to do your autopsy reports. Anyway, is Mister Babbit pleased to be here?'

'It's a cuddly toy,' Simple replied.

No one stepped into his world without an invitation.

'Is there any biscuits left?' he asked Aria.

'We've got drinks and nibbles today.'

Everyone sat down, poured themselves drinks and chatted, but each of them kept half an eye on Simple. First he took a pretzel, tasted it, said 'Poo-poo' under his breath and put it back in the bowl, then he bit into a cheesy biscuit, said 'Yuck' and put that back in the bowl too.

'Hey, hang on, he can't try them all!' protested Enzo.

'You're just about as disgusting as he is,' said Aria.

'What?'

'When you eat Nutella straight from the pot!'

At this point Simple was spitting a salted almond out into an ashtray, going: 'Pfft, pfft, pfft.' This was the last straw for Enzo.

'God, he's repulsive!'

Kleber unceremoniously grabbed his brother by the sleeve and forced him to his feet.

'I haven't tried all the nibbles!' Simple wailed indignantly.

'Come into the bedroom. You're not being very

nice. Come on, get your backpack and come with me.'

The brothers' exit was followed by an embarrassed silence.

'Well, no one said it would be easy,' Corentin couldn't help saying.

Chapter 3

*Where Mister Babbit wants
everyone to have a willy*

Simple was an early riser. Kleber had taught him to wait in bed, looking at picture books, but on this particular day, the wonderful world of flatsharing beckoned and Simple couldn't stay still. Without really meaning to, he ended up out in the corridor, barefoot and in his pyjamas. The whole apartment was bathed in the blessed torpor of the early morning. Realising that everyone was asleep, Simple said '*Shh*' to himself. He carried on halfway down the corridor. The silence was frightening. He ran back to his room and bounded on to his bed.

'What did you see?' asked Mister Babbit.

'Nothing.'

It was terrifying.

'Will you come with me?' asked Simple.

'Or we could make a cave?'

But Simple was tempted by the unknown. He grabbed Mister Babbit by the ears and went back into the corridor. He tiptoed along and came to a stop outside a closed door. There were mysterious sounds emanating from inside. Simple pressed his ear to the door and decided it could be one of two things: either there were two dogs fighting on the bed or the lil'men from the entry-phone were bouncing on the mattress. Simple resisted the temptation to look through the keyhole and headed on towards the living room.

He gave a triumphant 'Ah-ha!' when he spied the remains of their aperitifs on the coffee table. There were some little cubes of cheese that his brother hadn't given him time to try. He took a chilli-flavoured one out of its packaging and flattened it on the roof of his mouth. He went red in the face and couldn't spit the spicy mush out fast enough.

'That's poison! Poison!' cried Mister Babbit, hopping about the room. 'Here, drink this!'

He nudged the bottle of whisky towards Simple,

who poured himself half a glass and started drinking it. He thought he would suffocate.

'You're going to die!' Mister Babbit gasped enthusiastically.

Simple ran to the kitchen, turned on the tap and bent his head down to drink. When he stood back up, he failed to turn off the tap. He had just spotted something very interesting.

'A fire,' he told Mister Babbit.

There was a lighter next to an ashtray. Simple touched it with the tip of his finger, expecting a flame to spring up.

'Pick it up, pick it up!' Mister Babbit encouraged.

'There isn't a lil'man inside, is there?'

''Course not! He'd be all burnt.'

Simple looked up at the ceiling as he picked up the lighter. He didn't want to see what his hand was doing, because Kleber was bound to disapprove. He felt so guilty that the sound of a door opening made him jump. He slipped the lighter up his sleeve and tried to head back to his room. But the apartment was big and Simple went the wrong way, straight towards the bathroom, where Aria had just gone in, half draped in a T-shirt of Emmanuel's. Thinking that everyone else was still asleep at seven o'clock, she never bothered to lock the door. She stepped into the bathtub, turned on the taps, picked up the shower head and . . . screamed. Simple had opened the door.

'What the hell are you doing here? Get out!'

Simple looked at her, his eyes almost popping out of his head.

'Haven't you got a . . . willy?'

With one hand, Aria shielded herself like a classical Eve caught naked by sin.

'Or is it at the back?' Simple blundered on, incredulous.

By way of an answer, Aria pointed the streaming water at Simple, who beat a retreat.

'She got me all wet,' he said, really annoyed.

'Me too,' said Mister Babbit.

They both ran to the other end of the apartment and barricaded themselves in their bedroom.

'She's nasty,' said Simple.

But that was not what was bothering him.

'Did you see? She hasn't got a willy.'

'That's girls for you,' said Mister Babbit, lying down on the pillow.

54

'Don't they have willies?'

'No.'

Simple was very perturbed.

'Maybe just a little one? That you can't really see . . .'

'A titchy one?' Mister Babbit wondered.

Simple was not much given to speculation. He abandoned this delicate subject and shook his pyjama sleeve. He admired his loot and went to hide it under a sweatshirt in his wardrobe.

When Emmanuel came into the kitchen, he immediately noticed that the tap was running.

'Typical Enzo,' he said, turning it off.

The thought of his young rival brought a sneer to his face. He had just made love to Aria. He felt invincible. He knew he would soon be an intern in a Paris hospital, he would marry Aria and have children. Meanwhile, Enzo would still be a loser.

He made the coffee, counting out spoonfuls.

'. . . 5, 6 . . .'

'12, 9, B, 1000, 100.'

Startled, Emmanuel turned round.

'Oh, it's . . . um, it's you.'

He reluctantly addressed Simple directly. He would rather have referred to him in the third person, kept him at a distance, in some retard-land.

'Have you, um, taken your medicine this morning?'

'Medsun's not nice.'

There was a note of hostility in Simple's voice. Emmanuel reminded him of Malicroix.

'Oh, he's in here, is he?' Aria said as she came in.

Emmanuel felt relieved.

'Enzo forgot to turn the tap off,' he said.

'Enzo? Really?'

Aria looked questioningly at Simple.

'It wasn't me, it was Mister Babbit.'

'Good of him to take the rap,' Emmanuel said snidely, putting in another two spoonfuls before adding: 'So what do you think of our new flatmates? I think the casting is awful, don't you?'

Aria gesticulated that one of them was in room.

'It's OK, you can talk,' Emmanuel authorised her, 'he's a retard.'

'I-di-ot,' Simple corrected.

'He understands everything we're saying,' Aria protested.

Emmanuel and Aria sat down for breakfast, no longer distracted by Simple. They made some toast, asked each other for 'the butter, darling' and 'the jam, baby'. Simple, who was hungry, tried his luck with Aria.

'A biscuit, darling.'

She burst out laughing and went to get the tin of biscuits from the cupboard.

'Here, baby.'

'I'm not a baby. I've got a knife.'

Emmanuel slammed his cup down, muttering, 'I don't believe this.'

'Oh, calm down,' Aria said. 'He's OK.'

'Really? D'you think so?'

'Yes, I think so.'

They glared at each other.

'The lady's very nice,' Simple told his biscuit. 'But she still hasn't got a willy.'

Emmanuel stood up.

'I can't take this. I . . . I'm going to the bedroom.'

It was weird. Emmanuel was so confident, but Simple really threw him. Aria finished her breakfast alone while Simple played quietly with three spoons. The two soup spoons were mummy spoon and daddy spoon. The teaspoon was the baby spoon.

'You're an i-di-ot,' the daddy spoon told it. 'I don't want you here any more.'

Aria had been sitting musing sulkily, but now she listened to Simple's game.

'The mummy spoon's dead and the daddy spoon, he's put the baby spoon in an intistution. That can be the bowl.'

Simple plunged the small spoon into the remains of a bowl of coffee.

'Help! I'm sinking! Glug, glug, I'm sinking . . . The baby spoon was gonna die at Malicroix and the brother took him to a different house . . .'

Simple looked for something on the table. He caught sight of a spoon next to Aria's bowl. He walked two fingers towards it and peered up at Aria.

'I need the spoon,' he said very quietly.

She handed it to him. Simple gave a wide smile.

'It's the brother,' he explained.

'Is he going to go and get the baby spoon from the institution?'

Simple nodded, looking so happy that it brought tears to Aria's eyes.

'Do you like it here?'

He nodded again.

'It might grow, though,' he said.

'What are you talking about?'

'Your willy.'

Enzo was not an early riser. But Aria and Emmanuel's amorous antics had roused him from his slumber once again. He listened, tossed and turned in his bed, tried reading a bit, then got up, furious.

Enzo had a secret garden: an exercise book with squared paper, a place where he took refuge. When he was fifteen, he wrote poems, and Corentin thought they were brilliant. At seventeen, he had branched out into humorous novels, and Corentin thought they were wicked. At the moment, he was writing a novel, and hadn't told anyone about it. Round eleven o'clock he came out of his room, famished and headachy, having added half a chapter to his text. It was about a boy who made love by proxy, listening to the people in the next room.

'Good morning, Winnie,' Simple greeted him in the living room.

'Hello, village idiot. Actually my name's Enzo really.'

'My name's Simple really.'

'You know about banter,' Enzo conceded, sinking into the sofa. He cleared the cushions of the mess Simple had made, flinging it all off with the back of his hand.

'Do you think Kleber's dead?' asked Simple.

'Isn't he up?'

Simple shook his head.

'Maybe he's only dying,' Enzo soothed.

Simple picked up a Playmobil character from the floor. 'This is the cowboy.'

'Yup. I used to have all those guys in blue tunics,' Enzo remembered. 'They're the best.'

'No, the sheriff is.'

'No, the Blue Tunics.'

'The sheriff.'

They looked at each other. Simple wouldn't give in.

'You're a bloody pain, aren't you?'

'Uh-oh, bad word.'

Enzo lolled his head back on the sofa with a tired laugh.

'I want Kleber,' said Simple, worried. Enzo got

up, thinking the younger brother was pushing his luck leaving the other flatmates to look after the idiot.

'Come on, let's go and wake him up.'

Kleber was asleep. It was the first time for many nights that he had slept peacefully. Simple leapt on to his bed and shook him. Kleber sat up, dazed, fumbling for his glasses. He saw Enzo.

'What's the time?'

'Ten o'clock.'

Kleber took his watch from the bedside table. Almost midday.

'Bollocks!'

'Uh-oh, bad word,' Simple and Enzo said in unison.

They left Kleber to get dressed and went back to the living room. The front door slammed. It was Corentin.

'I went to buy another lighter,' he told Enzo. 'I don't know what I've done with mine.'

He glanced at Simple.

'Is he OK?'

'Yup, he's starting my education all over again,'

replied Enzo, patting Simple on the shoulder. 'It's a big job, isn't it?'

Simple sucked through his teeth.

It was a lovely day, so Kleber decided to take his brother for a walk. An old man was standing at the bottom of the stairs, one hand on the banister, the other holding a walking stick. He seemed to be waiting for the two brothers.

'You've blocked that rubbish chute again!' he railed. 'I'm going to tell the committee. I've had more than enough of this!'

Kleber raised his eyebrows and said nothing.

'Oh Lord, these ones are new!' the old man said angrily. 'How many of them are there in that apartment?'

Kleber thought it was best to ignore this rant, but Simple said very loudly, 'He's got a walking stick, he has. He'll be dead soon!'

Kleber stifled a burst of laughter and nudged his brother towards the door.

'We're going to do the shopping for the apartment, Simple. We're out of coffee and fruit juice.'

'Orange.'

To Simple, fruit juice was orange, ice cream was vanilla, and noodles came with ketchup.

'Do you think I'm going to die too?' Simple wondered.

'You're only little.'

'But what about when I'm bigger . . .'

Kleber smiled.

'You'll always be little. But everyone dies one day. With you it won't be for years and years.'

'Twelve?'

'More than twelve years.'

'1000, 20, B, 100?'

'Pretty much.'

Simple contemplated this information.

'What about you, when are you going to die?'

'I've no idea. Do you mind if we change the subject?'

Simple wanted to have a conversation like grown-ups.

'Do you know about girls, Kleber?'

Kleber mused that he would like to know more about them.

'Are you thinking about Aria? How pretty she is, is that it?'

Simple didn't answer. His brother didn't seem to know about the problem with girls. They went into a shopping centre. Outside the supermarket a security guard in a peaked cap stood with his legs apart and his hands crossed in front of his flies as if fearing an assault on that part of his anatomy.

'He's a soldja,' Simple said, pointing at him.

'Stop pointing at people.'

A little further on Simple started dragging his feet. They were passing the shelves of children's books.

'I'm not buying anything,' Kleber warned.

Simple stopped, his eyes popping.

'What are you looking at?'

Simple showed him a candy pink book with a picture of two rabbits apparently sulking, back to back, their arms crossed. Kleber read the title quietly: '*My Little Bunny in Love*.'

One of the two sulkers was in fact a girl. Simple put his finger on her. 'She's a girl rabbit.'

Kleber pulled his brother by the sleeve but he had taken root.

'She's a girl rabbit,' he said again as if it really mattered.

Kleber sighed and leafed through the book. The last picture showed the two rabbits in a tender embrace.

'I don't know if it's for your age group,' he said, half seriously.

Once back at the apartment, Simple ran to his room. 'Mister Babbit! I've got a rabbit book!'

'Let's see, let's see!'

First Simple closed the bedroom door, then he put the story in front of Mister Babbit.

'It's *My Little Bunny in Love*,' he said.

Mister Babbit leapt in the air. 'A Mrs Babbit, oh wow!'

'You're in love,' Simple teased him.

Mister Babbit smothered Mrs Babbit on the cover with kisses.

'Are you making love to her?' Simple asked.

They looked at each other. In real life things didn't seem that simple.

And everything got even more complicated towards the end of the afternoon when the elderly neighbour from downstairs rang at the door.

'Mr Villededieu,' Enzo greeted him urbanely. 'How is Mrs Villededieu?'

The neighbour rebuffed him with a 'That's enough from you!' and added, 'You've gone and blocked up the rubbish chute again. I've already told you not to put anything bulky down it.'

He came in, pointing his walking stick at Enzo – anyone would think he didn't really need the thing.

'Where's that rascal who wanted me dead earlier? Don't lie to me, I know he lives here!'

He scanned the room.

'I'll complain to the committee. Ah, now look who's here!'

This was how he greeted Aria, who had been drawn to the living room by his ranting.

'There, he's the one!' he cried, spotting Simple. 'I warn you, either you apologise or I'll lodge a complaint with the committee.'

Kleber intervened. 'My brother has learning difficulties. He didn't mean to offend you.'

'A madman!' yelped Mr Villededieu. 'You haven't any right to keep him here! This is a respectable building. He'll set the place on fire!'

Simple watched him, wide-eyed. How did he know he had stolen the lighter? His name meant 'city of

God', and Simple was sure that this man must have terrifying powers.

'Look, he's retarded,' Enzo said irritably, 'not mad.'

'I-di-ot,' Simple added very quietly.

'And it's none of your business, anyway,' added Aria.

'We'll see about that, young lady. There's a committee meeting next week. I can assure you I'll mention this.'

Once he was back out on the stairs, Mr Villededieu thought through all the boys he had seen in the apartment so far and came up with five. Five boys for one girl. Had they set up a rota?

'I'm going to kill him, I am!' said Simple after their neighbour had left. 'I've got my vevolver.'

He took the revolver from his pocket. Aria, Corentin and Enzo jumped.

'Hey, hang on, where the hell did he get that from?' asked Enzo.

'It's a toy,' Kleber explained, rather embarrassed. 'It's not dangerous.'

Enzo reached out his hand to Simple. 'Let's have a look.'

'You have to give it back after.'

Enzo adopted a knowing expression as he weighed the weapon in his hand, then pretended to take aim at Aria, for a long, long time, the revolver at arm's length.

'That's enough, OK?!' she said irritably.

He had a furious urge to shout, 'You'll see, I'll get you!'

But he lowered his arm. It wasn't as simple as that.

Chapter 4

Where Mister Babbit goes to church
but forgets to come back

On Sunday morning Corentin was astonished to see Simple and Kleber all dressed up.

'Where are you off to?'

'To Mass.'

'Does that still exist?'

He had a vague idea that church had been phased out along with cod liver oil and caning.

As they headed down the stairs, Simple asked if they really had to go.

'Yes,' replied Kleber.

'Is it long?'

'An hour.'

'An hour? Is that like twelve?'

'One hour's like one hour.'

Kleber never said much on Sunday mornings. The two brothers arrived late for Mass and snuck into the last pew. For a few minutes, Simple trotted out a random selection of 'Amen's and 'Happy-Luia's.

'Hallelujah,' Kleber corrected. 'And they don't expect you to join in quite so much.'

Then two people arrived even later than they had: an elderly man with a walking stick and a plump, considerably younger woman.

'Go on, then, go on,' she whispered, bundling her elderly husband into the pew.

Simple stood on tiptoe to tell Kleber, 'It's Mister God.'

Kleber nodded and smiled. Mr and Mrs Villededieu settled into the pew in front of them, and the old man shot them a passing glance that showed a mixture of surprise and fury. What was that idiot doing in amongst all these normal people? And since when had the young been going to Mass?

'It's really long,' sighed Simple.

'It's only just started.'

'Can I go and look at the picture.'

He pointed at an imposing painting, all gloomy

colours, depicting the Descent from the Cross. When he asked a third time, Kleber gave in: 'Go on. You're such a sodding pain.'

'Uh-oh . . .'

'Yeah, yeah, I'll go to confession. Now buzz off.'

Mr Villededieu looked round at them to make it clear they were disturbing him. Then he watched where the idiot boy went. Simple headed for the side aisle and stood in front of the painting for a long time, studying the Christ figure's tortured body, the marks left by the nails in his hands and feet, the hole from the lance in his side, and the trails of blood from the crown of thorns.

'Yucky poo-poo,' he murmured, fascinated.

Then he noticed the confessional. These little wooden cabins had intrigued him for some time. He popped his head through the curtain.

'No one there,' he said very quietly.

He slipped inside and sat on the little step where the penitent knelt. Then he took Mister Babbit from his pocket.

'Pfff, Mass is really long! Where are we, then?'

Mister Babbit looked round and seemed very excited.

'It's a cave! Let's play!'

After a few minutes, the organ started blaring up into the rafters and Simple thought how angry Kleber would be with him.

'Wait there, Mister Babbit. I'm going to do a bit of Massing, then I'll be back.'

'I'll keep your place,' replied Mister Babbit, only too pleased to be missing the tedious service.

Kleber looked very annoyed when his brother came back to sit next to him.

'Don't go out of sight! Where were you?'

'In the cave.'

Kleber shrugged one shoulder and forbade his brother any further distractions. Simple felt enormously happy when Mass was over.

'It wasn't long,' he said with some satisfaction, having spent the last quarter of an hour kicking the pew in front.

For his last afternoon of freedom, Kleber took his brother on a bateau-mouche along the River Seine and stopped him from drowning himself – three times – then they went to have an ice cream at the famous Berthillon. At Simple's request, the salesgirl listed all

the flavours: 'Passion fruit, guava, honey-nougat, cap-
puccino . . .'

Simple chose two scoops.

'Vanilla and vanilla!'

That evening, the Maluri brothers had supper alone
at the apartment. All the others were out having fun.
Once he was in his bedroom, Kleber set his alarm for
seven o'clock and got his bag ready – pens, paper,
timetable – with a heavy feeling in his stomach.
Someone knocked on the door.

'Aren't you going to bed, Simple?'

He shook his head.

'Mister Babbit hasn't come back yet.'

'What?'

'Mr Babbit. When's he coming back?'

'Oh, don't tell me you've . . .' Kleber paled. 'Have
you lost your Babbit?'

'Mister Babbit,' Simple corrected. 'I want him to
come back now.'

Kleber found it difficult to swallow. He had just
realised that the rabbit had not put in an appearance
all afternoon.

'Have you looked everywhere? He's not somewhere
in all your stuff?'

'He's in church.'

'In wh—'

Kleber muttered, 'My God,' which was apt.

'But where?' he cried. 'Where in church?'

'In the cabin.'

Kleber brought his hand to his brow to concentrate. 'The cabin? . . . The confessional! You put him in there, did you?'

Kleber muttered, 'Oh, fuck.' But Simple didn't have the heart to protest. He was very upset.

'Why won't he come back?'

Kleber exploded, 'Yes, I wonder why! He knows you can't sleep without him!'

'He's not being very nice,' Simple said reproachfully.

Kleber started pacing up and down mumbling to himself.

'What the hell am I going to do? What?'

Even if some child hadn't picked up the toy, the church would be closed for the night. Simple was going to have to do without Mister Babbit.

'We'll have to see tomorrow. I'll go to the church. Tonight you'll have to sleep without . . .'

He was so concerned by the expression in Simple's eyes that he couldn't finish his sentence.

'You'll just have to have the cowboy.'

Tears tumbled from Simple's eyes, and down his cheeks.

'I want him to come home.'

'I'm really sorry, but it's just not possible. Because he's not a real rabbit. He hasn't got legs, he can't walk. He's a toy!'

Kleber was shouting by the end, panicked by his brother's distress. Simple put his hands over his ears and ran to his room. Kleber chewed on his fingers, calming himself down. It was ridiculous to get in such a state over a cuddly toy. But when he ran his hand over his eyes he realised he was crying. This was awful.

Knock, knock, someone was at his door. He sniffed.

'Yes?'

It was Enzo.

'Hi . . . Is something wrong?'

Kleber didn't reply but opened his eyes wide with amazement. In Enzo's hand, right there, was Mister Babbit!

'Where did you find him?'

'Well, it's weird, he was out on the landing.'

'On the landing?'

75

'Yes. Seems he was too short to reach the door-bell.'

Enzo was telling the truth. He had just found the toy on the doormat. Kleber's first impulse was to rush into his brother's room, crying, 'Here he is.' But he changed his mind. He took Mister Babbit from Enzo, then went to knock on Simple's door.

'Go away! You're mean!'

Kleber opened the door a crack and peeped the rabbit's head into the room.

'Hello-o!' said Mister Babbit, waggling his ears.

'He's come home!'

Simple, who had been huddled in a corner, rushed over to his toy and hugged it to him. Kleber could go to sleep with the very picture of happiness engraved on his heart.

When the door was closed, Simple lay Mister Babbit down on the pillow.

'Why did you stay in church?'

There was a note of reproach in the question.

'To see it at night,' Mister Babbit boasted.

'What's it like?'

'Very dark.'

'With monsters?'

'A few.'

Mister Babbit was very brave.

'But you won't go off at night again?'

'Never again,' promised Mister Babbit. 'And you won't leave me in the cabin again?'

Simple shook his head. They had both been frightened. Simple without Mister Babbit was like Mister Babbit without Simple: the end of the world.

Simple may have slept the sleep of the blessed, but Kleber had a sleepless night. Was it the prospect of going back to college or the fact that Mister Babbit had come home on foot that kept him awake?

The following morning, Kleber prepared to leave his brother. Although he now recognised Mister Babbit had a degree of autonomy, he would have liked Simple to have a bit more company. He found Enzo in the kitchen.

'You're up early.'

'Not my fault,' Enzo grumbled.

'I'm off to college.'

No reaction. Enzo drank his coffee.

'Are you here this morning?'

'Where else would I be?'

'Would it bother you if . . . everything'll be fine . . . but if you could just keep an eye on my brother?'

'There's no sign saying "nurse",' he said, pointing at his forehead.

Kleber didn't say another word. It was wrong to ask for help from the flatmates. It could antagonise them.

''S OK,' Enzo drawled, 'I'll look after your idiot for you.'

And with that Kleber realised that Enzo was kind, but didn't want everyone to know about it.

Back in his room, Enzo tried to carry on with his chapter. But in his head he followed Aria's every move. She's having breakfast, she's writing the shopping list, she's putting on some lipgloss, Emmanuel's kissing her.

Enzo imagined it was him kissing her, not Emmanuel, and pressed his fist up to his mouth.

'This isn't getting any better,' he commented out loud.

He stretched and decided to go and have a chat with the idiot to clear his mind.

Simple had set his things up in the living room. He

liked playing on the carpet between the armchair and the sofa. All the Playmobil cosmonauts were having a day out. Facing them stood an army of lead and plastic: cowboys, Indians, Napoleonic soldiers, Goths and GIs. Simple, who was lying on his stomach, looked up at Enzo and beamed at him.

'It's war!'

Enzo slumped into an armchair.

'Who's winning?'

'The Heroes,' replied Simple, pointing at the cobbled-together army.

'What are the others called?'

'Malicroix.'

Simple got up on to his knees and shuffled closer to Enzo to confide, 'We're trashing Malicroix.'

'You don't hold back, do you?'

'What about you?'

'Me? I'm scared of everything. Even girls.'

Simple looked at Enzo. Did he know? He moved a bit closer, still on his knees, and said very quietly, 'You know girls, they haven't got willies.'

Enzo sat speechless for a moment, probably struck dumb by this revelation.

'Are you sure?'

Simple nodded.

'I saw Aria with nothing on.'

Enzo jumped.

'Really? Where was that?'

'In the shower.'

'Oh, doesn't she lock the . . .' and without finishing his sentence he let out an 'Ooooh': Simple was opening up new horizons for him.

'Enzo!' Aria called.

Enzo said, 'Ssh!' to Simple and winked at him.

'I'm in the living room.'

She came in, wearing a very short skirt and unlaced trainers, and with her hair all over the place. She may not have realised the effect she produced, but she did know she took Enzo's breath away when she appeared in front of him. But, to her, Enzo was just a kid and, to make matters worse, her brother's childhood friend.

'I haven't got time to do the shopping this morning. I know it's my turn . . .'

She gave an apologetic pout. Enzo watched her, open-mouthed.

'Could you pick up some Nutella and some cash? Specially now you eat it by the spoonful.'

'What, cash?'

Aria said, 'Ha, ha,' pointedly. 'Can you or not?'

'Not.'

'Too much work?'

'That's right.'

During this exchange, Simple swivelled his head back and forth, as if watching a tennis match, before deciding this was the time to extract a piece of information.

'How does making love work?'

The two of them burst out laughing. Then, the tension broken, Enzo murmured to Aria, 'You go. Your slave will do your bidding.'

Aria flushed and left the room, calling, 'Are you ready, Emmanuel?'

The two medical students left the apartment, and Enzo went to fetch his exercise book. He wanted to force himself to write every day, and felt that having an idiot for company would be an excellent stimulant. Simple went back to his game.

'One of the Heroes is very strong and he's prisoned a Malicroix.'

The very strong Hero was a mounted Gaul warrior, and Simple made him gallop across the carpet.

De-de-lum, de-de-lum, de-de-lum. Enzo looked down at his book. It would be the story of an idiot, an idiot discovering love . . . An hour later, Enzo was still writing, his hand galloping across the page.

'You're doing a lot of writing,' said a voice very close by.

Still kneeling, Simple was resting his elbows on the armchair, watching Enzo's pen scuttle along. Enzo leant towards Simple and knocked his head gently with his own forehead.

'Dong,' said Simple playfully.

'Did you know you're my friend?' whispered Enzo.

'Yup,' Simple whispered back.

Kleber was in lessons. He tried to keep focused but his thoughts kept straying. Please don't let Simple do anything terrible! What if he drives Enzo up the wall?

'We are particularly intractable on the subject of absenteeism,' said the physics teacher. 'Every absence will have to be justified.'

Handy if you don't live with your parents, thought Kleber. His timetable had already made him wince. On Mondays and Tuesdays he wouldn't get home till six.

After his little speech, the teacher called on each student to give his or her date of birth and chosen option.

To Kleber's right, a girl who was not yet seventeen said she was doing Greek. Her name was Zahra. Kleber followed the line of her profile as if intending to commit it to paper: slightly rounded forehead, a curve to her nose, dark lips, a strong chin. Which corner of the Orient was she from? Kleber, who had a romantic soul, dreamed of souks and harems.

'Maluri?' the teacher called. 'Kleber Maluri? Is he not here?'

'Yes, yes, I am!' Kleber jolted back to reality.

The other students started laughing at him. Zahra turned her pale grey gaze on him. She was not laughing, but her mouth bloomed into a full-lipped smile.

At the end of the lesson, Kleber noticed another girl, a round-cheeked redhead using both her hands to lift a cascade of hair that was making her hot. He wanted to touch her, but settled for staring at her. He thought about his brother's words: *Do you know about girls, Kleber?* No, he didn't know. He couldn't wait to know: he wanted to know the redhead's name and where Zahra was from, and to have their phone numbers, and to have a date with them, and – oh shit! He didn't even have time to think about it. He started running back to the Rue du Cardinal Lemoine.

In the hallway someone who was about to step into the lift let go of the door and turned towards him.

'Oh, is it you?' said Mr Villededieu. 'How's the idiot, then?'

Kleber almost told him to get lost, but the old man went on, 'I bet he was happy to be reunited with that filthy toy of his, wasn't he?'

'How do you mean?'

Mr Villededieu explained that he had seen Simple playing in the confessional. After Mass, Mrs Villededieu had wanted to light a candle to Saint Thérèse of Lisieux, whose statue was close to the confessional, and he had noticed the rabbit's ears peeping out.

'We got home late. I put the rabbit on the landing so as not to disturb you.'

Kleber fell over himself thanking their neighbour, slightly disappointed that the mystery of Mister Babbit had such a banal explanation.

He went into the apartment full of heart-stopping apprehension. He had claimed that Simple coped well with being on his own. In fact, he had no idea whether he would.

'Simple?'

He was in the living room, playing horses with Enzo.

'I can count!' bellowed Simple. '1, 2, 3, 4, B, 12!'

'We're making progress,' said Enzo, seriously exhausted.

What did the flatmates on the Rue du Cardinal-Lemoine dream about that night? Kleber shared himself fairly between Zahra and the redhead, Simple triumphed once again over Malicroix, Mister Babbit found a Mrs Babbit, and Enzo waited for dawn. Emmanuel was as punctual as a Swiss cuckoo clock.

'Seven o'clock,' sighed Enzo.

His disgruntled face soon broke into a smile. He got up and got dressed ... but not completely. Boxers and a T-shirt. That was enough. He looked at himself in the wardrobe mirror and tidied his hair ... but not too much. Then he sat down cross-legged and waited a little longer. When he heard the door to the next room open, he went stealthily to his own door. He had to let Aria be slightly ahead of him. He followed her in his mind's eye. She's getting undressed, she's running the water, she's stepping into the bath.

'Go!' Enzo spurred himself on.

He crossed the corridor and arrived outside the bathroom door, and was suddenly very afraid of what he was going to do. Because he *was* going to do it, definitely. He could hear the running water on the other side. He pictured Aria under the shower. He opened the door.

'Oh, sorry . . .'

It was Emmanuel.

Chapter 5

*Where Mister Babbit parties too hard
and ends up on the operating table*

'I can't find my lighter,' said Corentin, sitting down opposite Enzo.

'Again?'

'I thought I'd left it in the kitchen . . .'

Corentin suspected Enzo was messing around.

'Anyway,' he said, changing tack to talk about his twenty-first birthday celebrations. 'Are we going to have this party?'

'You have to say "soirée". It's more sophisticated.'

'No one says "soirée" any more. You're at least two generations out of date. But you didn't answer the question . . .'

'Well, at least it's a chance to get slaughtered, but

who are we going to ask?' Enzo added, looking around the room as if his life were a desert.

That was all the encouragement Corentin needed.

'I've thought about that . . .' he said. He had actually already made a list of names, and he produced it from his pocket.

'There's Hubert and Jean-Paul, they have to come. Fred, he's a friend of Aria's, but he's OK. There's my cousin Alexei who's just back from London . . .'

'Hey, hang on,' interrupted Enzo. 'What the hell's this list?'

He snatched the piece of paper from Corentin.

'There isn't a single girl!' he cried in outrage.

'Whose fault is that?' Corentin yelled back. 'Going to clubs is lame. Chatting girls up in the street is lame. Getting it on with your friends' birds is lame.'

'Do people still say "birds"?'

'Don't change the subject. I've put on four kilos in a year. I don't have a girlfriend. So I eat.'

'You *have* got fatter actually. Maybe you should smoke more?'

The two friends exchanged a hostile look. They

liked each other a lot, they just found it harder and harder to put up with each other.

I get it now, thought Corentin. *Enzo's in love with my sister.*

'Listen, Enzo, I'd have been happier if Aria had chosen you, too, but that's just the way it is. We're not going to waste our lives, OK? If I were a Muslim, I'd give her to you . . .'

'You don't fancy converting, do you?'

They sniggered.

'Right, gotta find some girls,' said Enzo. 'Or this is going to be a disaster.'

'We could ask the boy,' Corentin suggested.

'Who? Kleber?'

'Apparently there are some fit girls in his class.'

'Hey, hang on, you can't go asking some kid to tout for girls for you.'

'Have you got a better solution?'

Enzo sat there gazing into space for a moment.

'No.'

Kleber was flattered when Corentin invited him to his birthday.

'You can bring your girlfriends,' Corentin added condescendingly.

'Oh, thanks!' Kleber said, beaming. 'Is it OK if I ask two?'

'Ask as many as you like.'

In a week, Kleber had had time to do some groundwork. The redhead was called Beatrice. She punched boys in the stomach, swore like a trooper and always felt hot. Zahra was from the Lebanon. In lessons, her pen scratched away right up until the bell went. Kleber felt he had a chance with both. He told them about the flatshare, made them laugh with his descriptions of the other students, said nothing about Simple. Then he invited them to Corentin's party.

'I'll have to find a new top,' said Beatrice.

'I'll have to ask my father,' said Zahra.

In the end, they both said yes.

The party was on a Saturday night. Aria started preparing things in the kitchen first thing in the morning.

'So,' she recapped under her breath, 'carrot and celery sticks with a dip, meatloaf and then strawberry cheesecake . . .'

'Have you remembered candles?'

Aria was startled. She hadn't heard Enzo come in.

'Your hair looks like a doormat,' he commented.

She was still in her pyjamas, unwashed, her hair unbrushed.

'God, you get on my tits.'

She turned her back on Enzo and broke an egg into a bowl. Enzo crept over and whispered in her ear, 'Are you sure that's not what you want?'

'That's enough.'

'Enough of what?'

'I love Emmanuel and he loves me.'

'Well, good for you,' said Enzo, his voice hoarse.

'Stop bugging me or there'll be trouble.'

'From Emmanuel?'

Without saying a word, Aria gesticulated for him to clear off. Enzo beat a retreat to his bedroom. After closing his door he smacked his forehead against the wall as punishment.

'Fuck, what a chicken!'

He should have taken Aria in his arms, pushed his luck. A few sobs shook his whole frame.

'Fuck, that hurts.'

He had grazed the skin off his forehead. But that wasn't what he meant.

Meanwhile, Kleber also had a problem. Zahra and Beatrice were coming and he hadn't told them about Simple. Kleber glanced at his brother, who was just finishing setting up his army on the bedroom floor. The Franks stood shoulder to shoulder with Napoleonic soldiers.

'You've got your history a bit muddled,' he said glumly.

'That one's the strongest Hero,' replied Simple, brandishing the Gaul warrior.

Kleber smiled in spite of himself.

'Listen, Simple, this evening the others are having some friends over . . .'

'Yeah! I'm wearing a tie!'

'No, no, you mustn't disturb them. You'd better stay in your room. But I'll bring you some cake.'

Simple's face darkened. He could sense something. As the day went on he became more aware of being sidelined. He watched the preparations: Enzo pushing back furniture to clear a dance floor, Corentin disappearing into every room to look for CDs, Kleber trying on all his T-shirts, Aria bringing home flowers, Emmanuel concocting a pretty-coloured punch. The atmosphere was feverish and Simple, who had nothing to do, had a knack for getting under everyone's feet. Mister Babbit was all over the place, on the pile of CDs or in the plate of carrot sticks (well, he was a rabbit, after all). In the end Kleber threw him in his brother's face.

'For God's sake, keep him out of the way!'

Simple shut himself in his room. Mister Babbit was terribly upset.

'I hate Kleber.'

'He doesn't want us to go to the party,' explained Simple, almost in tears.

'They're going to eat all the carrots.'

'We won't get any cake.'

'Or any punch.'

Mister Babbit had remembered what the pretty drink was called.

'And I want to dance,' said Simple.

'You don't know how to. *I* do. But I need Mrs Babbit.'

They sat in silence, privately chewing over their disappointment. All at once Simple's face brightened.

93

He smacked his forehead with the flat of his hand. Why hadn't he thought of it sooner?

'Cinderella!'

He would dress up as a prince and appear halfway through the party. As soon as they had decided, Simple and Mister Babbit became very, very cunning. They snuck to the kitchen and stole a big saucepan lid as the prince's shield. In amongst his toys, Simple had a Zorro cape and a crown left over from a Nativity play. Mister Babbit wore the tie just in case a Mrs Babbit had been invited to the ball.

The first guests arrived at eight. Hubert and Jean-Paul, with bottles. Then Alexei, Corentin's cousin, with his English girlfriend. Beatrice and Zahra came together. The former had found a top that really only covered her top, amply revealing her belly-button piercing. *A bit obvious,* thought Kleber. The latter had an asymetric black nylon dress, exposing one shoulder. *A bit cheap,* thought Kleber, who desperately wanted them to like him, but was keen nevertheless to maintain an independent mind. Aria had invited two girls from her course who wouldn't give her any competition.

'Where the hell does she get them from?' moaned Corentin, who was already stuffing his face at the buffet.

'At least Kleber's made an effort,' said Enzo, serving himself some punch. 'The Lebanese girl's tasty.'

'Do you think so? I like the redhead more.'

'There's more to get your teeth into,' conceded Enzo.

General morale was so low that Emmanuel almost looked like a live wire. Still, when half the punch had gone, the girls seemed to thaw out noticeably. They started laughing for no obvious reason and Beatrice hoisted up her hair, asking anxiously, 'Don't you think it's hot?'

Corentin put on some music in case anyone felt like dancing, proving that man never does give up hope.

'We should move on to the vodka,' Enzo said.

He personally wanted to get drunk. Maybe then he would have the guts to take on Emmanuel. For now though, he carried on drinking punch with a grim expression and a sour mouth. Meanwhile, Kleber was actually making some headway. He was the one getting the girls to drink. He wanted to get up close to Beatrice; the curve of her back was so tempting.

'Have you got any slow stuff?' he came and asked Corentin.

Just as he was about to ask the redhead to dance, Kleber lost his nerve and settled for one of the medical students, even though he'd thought, *What the hell is that?* when she had walked through the door. The girl blushed and accepted: she thought Kleber was totally cute with his little round glasses and his cheeky smile. As for Corentin, he plucked up the courage to ask Beatrice to dance. Zahra, having been abandoned, ploughed into the plate of celery sticks. So good for the figure. Enzo, furious that Corentin was dancing with a girl when he himself was abstaining, decided to chat up whoever came his way. For the next slow dance, he invited the medic Kleber had just been dancing with – she'd never had such success.

For the last ten minutes, although no one had noticed, Simple had been in the room, dressed as a prince with his saucepan lid, his cardboard crown and his Zorro cape. The music, the clink of glasses and the girl's clothes were enough for him to think the party was a real ball. But weren't they all forgetting the most important part?

'Hey! Prince Charming's arrived!'

Kleber, who was drinking at the time, nearly choked. He had been so preoccupied with his seductive manoeuvring that he had forgotten all about his brother. Everyone fell silent and turned to Simple, who was holding Mister Babbit by his tie.

'Who's playing the princess?' he asked.

Emmanuel rushed up to Kleber and offered to do the injection for Simple's medication. Kleber, dying inside, went over to his brother and took him by the sleeve.

'Come on, I forgot to give you any cake.'

He turned to the gathering, but more particularly to Zahra, and said, 'This is my brother. He has learning difficulties.'

'An i-di-ot.'

It was such a strange scene that everyone froze – not *Cinderella* now but *Sleeping Beauty*.

'OK, we can't stand here all night,' Enzo spoke up suddenly. 'Simple is cool. Tonight, he's Prince Charming. Far as I'm concerned, that's not a problem.'

Enzo poured Simple a big glass of punch and

said quietly to Kleber, 'Don't worry, I'll take care of him.'

He took Simple off into a corner of the room but, on the way, caught Aria's eye. He saw a note of surprise and thought, *You don't know me at all, Aria.* Which was hardly surprising because he didn't know himself either.

Simple sat on a stool and, with the rabbit at his feet, knocked back his pretty drink in one gulp.

'That's excellent,' he said.

Enzo went to get him a slice of birthday cake.

'Is it apple tart?' asked Simple, scrutinising his plate.

Enzo looked at the cheesecake with its strawberries and whipped cream.

'At first glance, I'd say no. But maybe it's an apple tart in disguise.'

Simple started laughing.

'You're funny, you are.'

He pointed shyly at Emmanuel. 'He's a wally, he is.'

Enzo crouched in front of Simple and said, 'You're not as stupid as you look.'

'I'm your mate.'

To celebrate the fact, they clinked their glasses together.

'It's ess . . . essellent,' stammered Simple, draining his third punch.

Kleber had trouble getting back into his stride after his brother's sudden appearance. He felt he was the subject of the prying stares that people didn't dare focus on Simple. Beatrice was the first to ask a question, 'Is he like this all the time?'

'He's been like this since birth, yes.'

'Congenital?'

The question was loaded, a congenital anomaly could affect other people in the family.

'No, accidental. They blamed it on some pills my mum took to minimise the risk of miscarriage . . .'

Kleber felt very uncomfortable and his voice petered out.

'I've got a little sister who has a problem, too,' Zahra breathed in his ear.

He thanked her with a nod. But his urge to seduce had sunk without trace. People gradually started dancing again. Corentin turned up the volume, so much in fact that it took the neighbours several rings of the bell to make themselves heard.

'However many of them are there now?' bellowed Mr Villededieu, coming into the living room. 'I'm going to complain to the committee!'

Kleber came over to the grumpy old man.

'It's Corentin's birthday. We should have warned you about the noise.'

Mr Villededieu softened.

'And is that idiot at the party too? Oh look, and little blondy's getting drunk.'

'Good evening, Mr Villededieu,' Aria greeted him. 'Can I offer you some punch?'

She handed him a glass. The old neighbour's eyes started twinkling beneath his bushy brows.

'Goodness me, how many of these have you had?' he asked her, leering.

'Oh, five or six over the evening, no problem,' Aria replied, meaning the punch.

'Five or six?' Mr Villededieu repeated, looking round at all the healthy young men.

Corentin dimmed the lights. Kleber, who had found his courage in the bottom of a glass, asked Zahra to dance. In the half-light, he stroked her naked shoulder. Then he begged himself to have the courage to kiss it. 'On five. One, two, three, four . . .'

'Stop it,' Zahra tried to cool him down.

I'm flirting, I'm actually flirting! Kleber thought, over the moon. Beatrice was watching them contemptuously. Kleber was just a kid. She had spotted Enzo and went over to him.

'Are you the loony-keeper?' she asked, gesturing at Simple.

Enzo didn't react.

'What's he got there? A rabbit?'

She picked it up by the tip of one ear.

'It could do with a wash. What a bag of rags!'

She dropped it.

'Can't you go and do your belly dance somewhere else?' suggested Enzo.

This unchivalrous reference to her piercing made Beatrice flounce off.

'She's not pretty, she isn't,' said Simple.

He picked up Mister Babbit and tried to get to his feet. He reeled.

'Why'm I falling?'

Enzo helped him up.

'It's nothing, you're just a bit shedded.'

He took Simple to his bedroom, then went off to his own room. He picked up his exercise book and started writing.

Meanwhile, Simple was emptying out his pencil-case, trying to find a pair of scissors.

'I don't want to be rags any more,' said Mister Babbit. 'You can cut them off.'

Mister Babbit had taken Beatrice's comments to heart and wanted his ears to be cut off. Simple, who was drunk, found Mister Babbit's request perfectly reasonable.

'Shall we just cut them a little bit or right off?' he asked.

'Right off.'

Simple wedged Mister Babbit between his knees. As there seemed to be four ears rather than two, he blinked several times. Then he started hacking into the toy.

'Does it hurt?'

'It tickles.'

Reassured by this, Simple snipped one ear clean off.

'Is it bleeding?' asked Mister Babbit.

'No.'

'Have to put some blood on it.'

Simple took the lid off a red felt-tip, then daubed some on his fingers and some on Mister Babbit on the site of the cut.

'What are you doing?'

Kleber, overcome with remorse, had come to see what his brother was up to. He stood there watching, speechless.

'It's Mister Babbit,' said Simple. 'He doesn't want to be rags any more.'

'Your rabbit! That's horrible!'

Kleber took the toy from Simple's bloodied hands.

'Where's the ear?'

He picked it up.

'Oh, this is horrible . . .'

Simple burst into tears.

'I don't want his ear to be cut off!' he wailed, suddenly grasping what he had done.

'What's going on?'

Kleber turned to the door. He was holding Mister Babbit in one hand and the ear in the other.

'Oh, Aria, look what he's done!'

The girl came closer.

'Poor Mister Babbit . . .'

'I did it,' sobbed Simple. 'I'm horrible!'

Aria leant towards him. 'It's OK, I'll sew it back on.'

She stood up and added, 'He's been drinking. Enzo gave him punch. I'll get my sewing bag.'

Kleber lay Mister Babbit on the pillow and waited nervously for Aria to come back.

'It's going to be OK, boys!' she said, seeing their miserable faces. 'I'm a med student. I know all about sewing ears back on.'

'Are you going to do the operation?' asked Simple.

He was already feeling better. Taking a keen interest, he watched Aria look for the right colour cotton, thread it through the needle, then push the needle into the toy. He said 'Ouch' under his breath.

'He's not in any pain,' Aria reassured him. 'I've anaesthetised him.'

She finished the stitching, then waggled Mister Babbit's ears, saying, 'Hello-o.' Simple clapped and Aria turned to Kleber.

'I'll stay. Till he's sobered up.'

Kleber protested that it was really his job to keep an eye on his brother.

'No, I want Aria. She's nicer than you.'

So Kleber went back to join the others, leaving Simple in Aria's tender care.

'How are you feeling?' she asked him. 'Is your head spinning?'

The question made Simple laugh; he didn't see how his head *could* spin. Aria was sitting on the bed, right next to him. It was the first time she had looked at him in his own right, and not as Kleber's brother. He was a frail young man with shambolic hair and eyes like magic lanterns that saw princes and pirates, unicorns and sprites.

'Simple,' she said.

'That's my name, that is.'

She stroked his cheek. He had skin like a child. He opened his eyes wide, amazed by this sign of tenderness. His mummy had died so long ago.

'Do you want me to kiss you?' asked Aria.

Just in case, he closed his eyes. She kissed him. He stank of rum.

'Will you kiss Mister Babbit too?'

He pressed the toy's nose up to Aria's lips.

'He's happy,' he said. 'He's got blood on him . . .'

Simple looked at the small red mark left by the

felt-tip at the base of his ear, apparently a bit annoyed about it.

'But he's happy.'

'Because of the kiss?'

Mister Babbit waggled his ears enthusiastically.

Chapter 6

*Where Mister Babbit makes
love and war*

Mister Babbit woke feeling as though he had a vice round his ears. Simple rubbed his temples.

'Does your head hurt?'

'It's spinning,' complained Mister Babbit.

The others can't have been in any better shape because, at gone ten o'clock, nothing was stirring in the apartment. Simple saw at least two advantages to this: there would be no Mass this Sunday, and he could go and explore the remains of the party at his leisure.

The living room was a bombsite. Glasses had been left all over the place, and the floor was strewn with bits of crisp and cake.

'A fire!' exclaimed Simple. Corentin had left his new lighter next to a brimming ashtray.

'For your collection,' said Mister Babbit as Simple snaffled it.

Rabbits are never short of wicked ideas.

'There's ciragettes,' said Simple casually. There were lots of them, some only half smoked.

'I know how to smoke,' Simple boasted.

He picked up one of the cigarette stubs delicately between his thumb and forefinger, and brought it to his lips, pursing his mouth tightly. Then he blew imaginary smoke up at the ceiling, perfectly imitating Beatrice. In more virile mode, he clamped another between his first two fingers and sucked on it like Corentin, who was doing his best to line his lungs with tar.

'Not bad,' Mister Babbit admitted. 'Are you going to light it now?'

Simple seemed less familiar with handling the lighter and, when the flame eventually sprang up, he dropped it. Spurred on by Mister Babbit, he succeeded in lighting his cigarette on the third attempt. He inhaled, then began coughing and spluttering, tears fogging his eyes.

'Is it good?' asked Mister Babbit.

'Excellent,' said Simple, coughing.

He smoked three butts like this, then felt very weird, his throat dry and his heart fluttering.

'You've gone all white,' Mister Babbit observed with some interest. 'And a bit green too.'

Simple clamped his hands on to his stomach, then his throat, and stammered, 'Kleber', before bending double and throwing up.

'Help, help!' cried Mister Babbit, hopping up and down, which was not particularly helpful.

When it was over, Simple stood there dazed.

'That's yuck, yuck,' said Mister Babbit in a nasal voice because he was holding his nose.

Panicked by the extraordinary thing that had just happened to him, Simple ran off, threw the door to his brother's room open and jumped on his bed.

'Kleber!' he screamed. 'I've been sick!'

Then, when his brother didn't react quickly enough to this astonishingly interesting piece of news, he shook him violently. 'I've been sick!'

Stunned, Kleber sat up, fumbling for his glasses on the bedside table.

'What? Where?'

'At the party. I was sick loads!'

Kleber threw back his sheets and got up, unsteady on his feet.

'You've got nothing on,' Simple criticised. You couldn't go around showing your knife like that.

Kleber pulled on a pair of boxers and hurried to the living room.

'Oh no,' he groaned.

It was right there, in the middle of the carpet.

'It stinks,' Simple commented.

Kleber had to clean the carpet, air the room and clean the carpet some more, all the while cursing his brother, who refused to help him. 'You're such a pain! Such a pain! I'm going to lose you in the woods. I can't take this any more!'

Simple blocked his ears but he could still hear, and terrible images loomed in his mind. It wasn't *Sleeping Beauty* now but *Snow White*.

The flatmates all got out on the wrong side of bed. Emmanuel announced that Simple's condition required confinement to a psychiatric hospital.

'He's already been put in an institution, if you must know,' Kleber exploded. 'My father farmed him out so he could remarry. Simple had learning difficulties

110

before but at Malicroix they drove him mad. He didn't react to anything any more. So I took him away from there. I told my father I'd take care of Simple. I'll never send him back to Malicroix, never. If you don't want him here any more, then you don't want me here any more. Well, fine. You go ahead with your little student lives paid for by the bank of Mum and Dad. And I hope it makes you happy.'

He left the kitchen, where everyone had gathered, and went to his room to pack. Simple joined him and watched, huddled in the corner of the room.

'Are you going to lose me in the woods?' he said in a very small voice.

'We'll get lost together.'

This news soothed Simple and he in turn wanted to reassure his younger brother.

'I've got my vevolver, I have.'

There was a knock at the door, it was Enzo.

'What are you doing?' he asked.

'It's pretty obvious. Packing.'

Enzo stood there for bit. Then he said, 'I've done some negotiating. Emmanuel was a bit stubborn. But in the end he agreed that you . . . both of you could stay.'

Kleber put down the books he had in his hand.

'You're very kind. But it's no use. He'll only blow a fuse tomorrow or the next day.'

'No, I don't think so. I cranked up the guilt factor. You did most of the work, I just laid on a bit more. "Selfish, middle-class . . ." I even called them "adults"!'

Kleber was touched. He was well aware of what the others were doing to help him and him alone.

'Anyway, it was my fault,' added Enzo. 'I shouldn't have got your brother drunk. I made him ill.'

Kleber was still undecided. Did he have any right to expect the other flatmates to help him without offering them anything in return?

'I'm going to tell you something, Kleber. I'm glad you two are here.'

Enzo pointed to Simple, who was still huddled in his corner with Mister Babbit. 'He's the most intelligent bloke I know.'

'You shouldn't point at people,' Simple scolded.

Enzo went over towards him with his hands on his hips and pretended to be angry. 'Right, you, you'd better shut your trap! You can't go around telling other people what to do when you just fuck up one thing after another. And don't say "Uh-oh, bad word!"'

'Well, my brother's going to lose you in the woods, he is!' Simple retorted, furious.

Enzo heaved a sigh and turned to Kleber. 'He's a sodding pain.'

'Uh-oh, bad word.'

At lunchtime Simple refused to eat and stayed in his room. Mister Babbit wasn't feeling well. He kept clutching his stomach and saying, 'Ow, ow,' and he was racked with hiccups and spasms.

'Are you being sick?'

'No, I'm spewgulping.'

Mister Babbit couldn't do anything normal like a human.

'I'm all hot with a fever,' he said. 'I need a doctor.'

Simple stood there thinking for quite a while. To get a doctor to come out you had to say, 'Hello, doctor, Mister Babbit's ill.'

'I haven't got a tephelone,' said Simple.

All of a sudden he smacked his forehead with the flat of his hand. Aria! Aria was a doctor.

Simple went to the living room, where Aria was ironing a shirt for Emmanuel. She watched warily as he came over. She regretted what she had done the night before.

''S Mister Babbit, he's ill,' he said.

Aria just managed a 'Hmm . . .' She didn't feel like playing the game.

'Can you give him some medsun?'

'Listen, I don't feel like . . .'

Aria frowned, put down the iron and put her hand on Simple's forehead. It was burning hot. His eyes were shining feverishly.

'You've got a hell of a temperature.'

She felt his glands in his neck, made him open his mouth and say 'Ah', and asked if his stomach hurt.

'Yes.'

'And your head?'

'Yes.'

'And your throat?'

'Yes.'

She looked at Simple closely.

'And your shoes?'

'Yes.'

114

She patted him on the cheek, half irritated, half amused.

'Come on. You need something to make you feel better. I'm thinking Ibuprofen.'

'Is it OK if I don't?' Simple asked shyly.

'What do you mean?'

'You said you'd buprofen but I don't know how to buprofen.'

Aria laughed: 'No, it's the medicine. It's called Ibuprofen.'

'Mister Babbit doesn't want any buprofen.'

Aria grabbed Simple by the shoulders. 'D'you want to know something. You're driving us mad with your Babbit.'

'Mister Babbit.'

'You do realise it's a toy, don't you?'

Simple blinked but didn't answer.

'Is it a real rabbit? Are you going to answer me?'

Simple had his revenge ready. 'It doesn't look nice not having a willy.'

Aria told Kleber that his brother might have an upset stomach. She played doctor and provided the medication. Simple spat the pills out and his temperature kept on rising. By late afternoon he was delirious. Kleber watched over him while he filled in administrative forms for college.

'We're in the woods,' said Mister Babbit. 'Kleber's a bastard.'

'Uh-oh –'

'Yes, but he's a bastard. He lost us in the woods. We're going to die. There's a witch.'

'Kleber!' Simple called, panicking.

Kleber put down his papers and came over to his brother.

'What's the matter?'

'It's the witch!' cried Mister Babbit. 'Go away, nasty witch, go away!'

'Go away!' cried Simple in unison with him.

'You really have got a high temperature,' muttered Kleber.

He put another pill into a glass to dissolve. But Mister Babbit was on the case.

'Beware the witch – she wants to give you a poisoned apple.'

'Here,' said Kleber, handing him the glass. 'And drink it this time.'

'No, it's poison!'

Simple lashed out at Kleber's arm and sent the glass flying across the room.

'You're a witch! I'm going to kill you, I am.'

The fever was making Simple's pale eyes burn.

'No improvement?'

Aria had just come in.

'He's hallucinating,' stammered Kleber. 'He thinks I'm a witch.'

'Maybe it's his way of externalising his fears,' said Aria, who was swotting up on Freud.

'I can hear the princess's voice,' said Mister Babbit. 'We'll be saved. Are you going to call to her?'

'Aria?' called Simple.

'You see, he's not all that bad,' said Aria. 'He recognised me.'

She leant over Simple, who closed his eyes.

'Are you OK? Simple, can you hear me?'

He opened his eyes again. 'But I'm the prince! Aren't you going to kiss me?'

Just then, a voice called from the corridor, 'Are you there, Aria?'

It was Emmanuel.

'I want the princess to kiss the prince,' Simple demanded.

Aria was torn.

'Close the door, quickly!' she whispered to Kleber.

Kleber did as he was told, then came back over to Aria.

'I . . . I did something stupid with your brother,' she admitted. 'Can you keep this to yourself?'

Kleber raised an eyebrow and a smile started twinkling in his eyes.

'Something stupid?'

'No . . . for God's sake, not that. I kissed him yesterday.'

Simple sat on his bed and screamed at the top of his lungs, 'I want a kiss!'

'Just shut up!' said Kleber.

Someone knocked on the door.

'Another ki—'

Aria shut Simple up by kissing him. Emmanuel popped his head round the door.

'Sorry, Kleber, I'm looking for . . . Oh, there you are!'

'Yup, yes,' said Aria, hurrying towards the exit. 'I came to see if his temperature had gone down.'

She dragged Emmanuel into the corridor. Mister

Babbit was jumping for joy on the bed. 'You're better,' he said. 'You're all better! The princess kissed you!'

The following morning, Kleber had a struggle to get out of bed and haul himself to college. Simple was feeling much better and Mister Babbit was fine. They both went to the kitchen, where they found Corentin looking for his lighter.

'I don't believe it,' he grumbled. 'What have I done with it?'

Tired of searching, he picked up the matches.

'You smoke ciragettes, you do,' Simple said admiringly. 'Are you going to be sick?'

'No,' replied Corentin, a little surprised.

'I'm sick.'

'It's because you're not used to it. Mind you, it's not worth getting used to. Smoking's bad for you.'

He noticed that Simple was listening attentively so he explained in his best teacher's voice.

'It causes serious illnesses like lung cancer.'

'Illnesses what you die from?'

'Yes. I had an uncle who smoked two packets a day and . . .'

Corentin fell silent, becoming aware of a fairly unpleasant fact: he smoked two packets a day.

'And what?'

'And he got lung cancer. He was not a pretty sight at the end.'

'At the end of dying.'

Corentin mumbled, 'Mm, yup,' and stubbed out his cigarette emphatically.

'All scrumpled,' Simple beamed before heading back to his room with some biscuits, leaving Corentin wondering how efficient nicotine patches were.

Simple made himself comfortable on his bed and looked at *My Little Bunny in Love* for the twentieth time. Previously, Mister Babbit had rushed to kiss the girl rabbit. This morning he sat sulkily in front of the book.

'Aren't you going to make love to her?' Simple asked, surprised.

'It's a picture. I want a real Mrs Babbit.'

Simple could find nothing to say to that.

'Mrs Babbit,' insisted Mister Babbit, 'do you know where she is?'

Simple thought for a long time, sitting cross-legged on his bed and rocking backwards and forwards. All of a sudden he smacked his forehead with his hand.

'The shop!'

On Monday evening Kleber was planning to head off after lessons to buy some bits and pieces of stationery. He dropped in on the apartment to take Simple with him because he liked the shopping mall.

'So, how's it going, lover boy?'

'It's not me, it's Mister Babbit,' said Simple.

'Yeah, yeah.'

Kleber started laughing. He loved stories about relationships and break-ups. He couldn't wait to experience them for himself.

When they reached the supermarket, Simple came to a stop in front of the security guard.

'There's not a war on,' he said.

Kleber was quick to drag his brother away by the sleeve.

'Don't talk to strangers.'

'I know him. He's the soldja.'

Simple slowed down; they were coming to an interesting aisle.

'I warn you, I'm not buying anything,' said Kleber.

'Hie han ha hi-hi ha-hi.'

'What?'

Simple stood on tiptoe and whispered in his brother's ear, 'I want a Mrs Babbit.'

'I haven't got any money,' Kleber said adamantly.

'You can just buy some.'

'That's a no. I'm going over to the stationery.'

'I'll just look at the toys.'

Kleber narrowed his eyes at Simple, then shrugged and left him there. As soon as he was alone, Simple looked through all the toys. He was tempted by the Playmobil characters in blue tunics, but shook his head to himself. He was here to look for a Mrs Babbit. He saw a monkey, a Mickey Mouse, a snake, he knocked down a small cow and apologised to it. He started playing with a big teddy and a smaller one.

'This is the daddy bear and this is the baby bear, he can be the idiot . . .'

Then he shook his head to himself again and carried on with his search. Next to the cuddly toys, a new range of products was on display: animals made of fabric, and dressed in retro outfits. Simple came to a standstill and smiled. There she was, Mrs

Babbit in a bonnet with two holes for her ears, and a pretty little apron over a gingham dress. Simple knew Kleber wouldn't want to buy her. He put her under his jacket, making sure her feet and ears were well tucked away.

'Don't move,' he told her under his breath.

Then he crossed his arms and waited for his brother to come back, looking so innocent that Kleber eyed him suspiciously.

'Come on, we can use the express till.'

Simple was disappointed by the express till. He had been hoping for something better than this normal-looking woman sitting behind a machine. When he walked past her, he set off a strident alarm and brought his hands up to his ears. As his jacket parted, Mrs Babbit fell to the floor at his feet.

'What the hell's that?' spluttered Kleber.

The security guard came over, rolling his shoulders.

'Look, it's stolen! He stole it!'

'Don't come any closer, soldja!' wailed Simple. 'I've got a vevolver!'

'You'd better come and explain yourself,' the guard bellowed in turn.

'He's got learning difficulties,' Kleber yelled even louder.

Simple took out his toy revolver. 'I'm going to war, I am!'

'A gun! Help!' screamed the cashier.

'It's a fake,' Kleber yelled again.

Customers were just beginning to panic when an elderly man parted everyone with his walking stick and intervened in a thundering voice, 'Stop all this nonsense! I know these boys. This one here with the rabbit's a halfwit. The other one, with the glasses, is a good lad. He blocks the rubbish chute but he goes to Mass. Now you put that away . . .'

This was addressed to Simple, who put his revolver away.

'It's Mr God,' he said with a wide smile.

'I'll, um . . . pay for the toy,' stammered Kleber.

He was so ashamed he could hardly breathe, and he fled, dragging his brother by the sleeve.

'You see, you have got some money,' Simple pointed out.

'I warn you,' replied Kleber, blinking away tears, 'Mister Babbit has got his Mrs Babbit, fine. But they won't be having any babies!'

When they were back at the apartment, Simple wanted to surprise Mister Babbit. He peeped the girl rabbit's head round the bedroom door. 'Hello-o!'

Mister Babbit sat up from the pillow.

'What's that?'

Simple closed the door behind him carefully.

'It's Mrs Babbit.'

'That? It's a stuffed toy.'

Simple looked at the fabric rabbit in amazement, then he flung her through the air. She landed on the far side of the room. Mister Babbit started laughing and Simple did too. She was a real twit.

The following morning, Corentin got up in a filthy mood. He had decided to stop smoking. He opened the fridge and took out what was left of the paté, salami and cheese, and sat down, barely glancing at Simple, who was dunking shortbread biscuits in orange juice. He sliced himself some bread and salami, buttered the bread, slapped some cheese on to it, poured himself a coffee, ate, drank and ate some more, barely giving himself time to breathe, let alone chew.

Simple, who was facing him, went, '*Oink, oink.*'

Corentin looked up and, with his mouth full, asked, 'What do you mean, "*oink, oink*"?'

'It's a pig. It goes *oink, oink*.'

No one had ever told Corentin so clearly that he ate like a pig. Slowly, he pushed his plate away.

'You really have to stick your nose in everything, don't you,' he said irritably.

He had put on another two kilos recently.

Chapter 7

*Where Mister Babbit narrowly
escapes the sharks*

Summer lingered on into September that year, and Beatrice often found she was hot at the end of lessons. Holding her bare arms high above her head, she coiled her hair into a scrunchy to get it off the back of her neck, and, as he watched the show, Kleber smiled and his eyes went all dreamy.

This particular day, Zahra was walking right past him and gave him a contemptuous look. It startled him.

'Are you leaving with us?' he asked her.

Zahra's gaze swivelled from Kleber to Beatrice.

'No thanks,' she said, walking away holding her backpack close to her heart.

'She turns her nose up at everyone,' Beatrice commented. 'Have you got time to walk.'

Kleber always seemed to be in a hurry.

'You worried your brother'll set fire to something?'

Kleber didn't like the way Beatrice talked about Simple.

'We can go along the river,' he suggested. 'We could talk . . .'

Beatrice talked about the boys and girls in their class. The boys were bloody morons and the girls were pathetic. Kleber let her talk, and kept wondering whether he should hold her hand. When she stopped on the bank to watch the boats, he thought about putting his arm round her waist. But her backpack would get in the way.

'Don't you think?' she asked.

'Yes, yes,' said Kleber, who hadn't been listening. 'Shall we go down the steps?'

He was hoping to find inspiration at the water's edge. Two lovers were kissing on a bench.

'Shall we sit down?'

They put their backpacks at their feet. *One problem sorted*, thought Kleber.

'What do you make of Zahra?' she asked.

'She's nice.'

'You think everyone's nice! Can't you see the way she looks at you like a love-sick puppy?'

Kleber didn't know what to say.

'She says her dad's strict. If she's that up for it the whole time, he needs to be.'

Kleber suddenly wished he was at home with Mister Babbit.

'Do you like girls who are up for it?' Beatrice said suggestively.

Kleber felt her pressing against him, her thigh, her arm, her shoulder. He wasn't the one controlling things here.

'You know, what I don't like about boys is that's the only way they see us. Our bums, our tits. You feel like you're just lots of bits and pieces strung together. D'you know what I mean?'

Kleber tried to protest: 'Actually, no, not all boys are like that. Of course some have a one-track mind, but boys can be romantic too.' He let out a sigh when he had finished. 'Right,' he added. 'I'd better go home now. My brother'll be worried.'

He picked up his backpack and peeled himself away from Beatrice, her thigh, her arm, her shoulder. They both stood up. *I must kiss her*, thought Kleber. His dignity as a male was at stake. *I'll count to five. One, two . . .* At three, she kissed him.

The least he could do was to hold her.

'You see, you're just like the others,' she said, pushing him away.

When Kleber said goodbye to her on the bridge, his penis felt like a knife digging into him.

'Simple!' he called, rushing into his bedroom.

His brother was sitting on the floor and looked up.

'Who's attacking you?'

Kleber had run all the way home.

'Is it the soldja?' asked Simple, leaping to his feet. 'I've got my knife.'

'Good, so've I.'

Kleber flopped into the armchair.

He buried his face in his hands.

'You dead?' Simple asked gently.

No reply.

'Hello-o . . .'

Kleber felt the rabbit's ears tickling his hands.

'Is that you, Babbit?' he said, softening.

He stroked the rabbit.

'Mister Babbit,' Simple corrected.

Kleber looked intently at his brother. He really wanted to confide in someone.

'Guess what, I kissed a girl. You saw her at the party. It's Beatrice.'

'She's not nice.'

Kleber was surprised by this quick-fire reply.

'No, that's not true. She's quite . . .' Kleber tried to find the word. Domineering? Aggressive? Castrating? What point was there using vocabulary like that with Simple? 'She wants to be in charge. And I don't know what I'm supposed to do, if I can't . . . be the man any more.'

He felt ridiculous saying this, and sniggered at himself. Then he let his head fall back against the chair, and closed his eyes.

Simple watched him for a long time before whispering, 'He's asleep.'

He moved away from his brother and, sitting on the floor, started playing with Mister Babbit. He picked up the girl rabbit by her skirt.

'This is Babbita,' he said. 'She's coming to see Mister Babbit. Knock, knock. Come in.'

Simple started doing two different voices, one deep and childish, the other higher and pretentious.

'Hello, Babbit.'

'Mister Babbit.'

'Well, yes, but I say Babbit because I'm in charge.'

'You're not pretty, anyway. You haven't got a willy.'

'Well, who needs one of those when I've got a pretty skirt. That's much better.'

'No it's not,'

'Yes it is.'

'No.'

'Yes.'

'They start fighting,' Simple commented, smacking the two rabbits together.

Kleber opened his eyes again.

'Babbita's winning,' said Simple. 'She's crushing Mister Babbit.'

The girl rabbit was on top of Mister Babbit, trampling his head. Kleber felt completely crushed.

'Hey,' said Mister Babbit. 'I can see under your skirt!'

Babbita gave a terrible scream and started pummelling Mister Babbit with her ears.

'You're such a pain!' Simple cried suddenly. 'Anyway, you're just a toy.'

He took the girl rabbit and hurled it against the

wall. Kleber burst out laughing, and Simple spun round to face him.

'You're not sad now?'

In the apartment on the Rue du Cardinal-Lemoine, somebody else was doing some soul-searching. Try as he might, Enzo couldn't see how to sell himself to Aria. Emmanuel was taller than him, more attractive, more mature, from a wealthy family.

'What does that leave me?' he said. 'I'm more of a laugh? Yeah, but it's a load of rubbish that you can get girls by making them laugh. They all want you to have a sense of humour but when you try to get them into bed what they really want is big pecs.'

'Come on, young man, come on, don't run yourself down!'

Mr Villededieu had come up to complain that they had blocked the chute again. Enzo had swiftly told him to take a hike, saying he had other things to worry about. Then one thing led to another and he ended up confiding in him.

'What's the name of this young lady who's resisting your advances?' asked Mr Villededieu in his slightly dated turn of phrase.

'Well . . . it's Aria!' exclaimed Enzo as if he expected the whole world to know.

'Aria? You mean the girl who lives here with you?'

Enzo nodded. 'What is it?' he grunted. 'Why are you looking at me like that?'

'But I thought . . . Isn't she *your* sweetheart?'

'Girlfriend, no. She's Emmanuel's girlfriend.'

The old man looked really amazed.

'But I thought . . .' he said, then lowered his voice to add, '. . . that she was everyone's girlfriend here.'

Enzo was horrified.

'Bloody hell! Is that what it was like in your day?'

Mr Villededieu admitted that he had interpreted things all wrong.

'So, she has no soft spot for anyone else?'

Enzo pulled a face.

'I'm pretty sure she likes Simple.'

'The halfwit? Well, in that case, you're in with a chance.'

'Thank you, Mr Villededieu.'

'Call me George. I didn't say that to upset you. If

your Aria can take an interest in another man, then why shouldn't she take an interest in you?'

'But she already knows I'm in love with her.'

'And?'

'And she couldn't give a damn.'

Mr Villededieu thumped the floorboard with his walking stick.

'Show her you're a man! And be rough, my boy!'

'What does that mean, then? Ramming her up against the kitchen sink?'

Enzo flushed in spite of himself; the thought had already occurred to him.

'You've got to make a stand,' Mr Villededieu hammered out his point. 'Tell her you can't bear life without her, you know, all the usual nonsense . . . and kiss her and . . .'

He hugged his walking stick to him. Enzo was still unconvinced.

'What are you afraid of?' the old man asked.

'A slap.'

'Being slapped by a woman you love is a memory to savour when you're old.'

'You've got some pretty whacky arguments, Mr Villededieu.'

'Call me George. And remember, be rough!'

'I should really go for it, then?' Enzo said, his voice cracking.

The way he was feeling, he might as well try.

Enzo had noticed that on Tuesday afternoons it was just Simple, Aria and himself in the apartment. So he had to make his move on a Tuesday afternoon. He was in a complete state on Tuesday morning. At lunchtime he couldn't eat a thing. By two o'clock he was wondering whether he wouldn't rather throw himself out of the window.

Aria was in the living room, sitting in a rather complicated way with one leg bent on the sofa, the other swinging freely, her T-shirt only half tucked into her jeans. She was reading a photocopied worksheet and sighing impatiently. Enzo sat down beside her. He was shaking.

'Is . . . is that something you need to learn by heart?'

She gave him a sideways glance.

'Scram.'

Enzo felt a surge of anger.

'Why do you talk to me like that? Because I love you?'

Just in time, he remembered George's advice.

'I don't want to live without you. I think about you day and night. Specially with sodding Emmanuel waking me up every morning!'

Enzo felt he was getting this all wrong, but he bull-dozed on. *And be rough, my boy!* He launched himself at Aria.

'I love you. I want you.'

He was not particularly surprised to earn a slap. But he hadn't expected Aria's hand to deliver quite such a heavy blow.

'Fuck!' he said, reeling.

'Uh-oh, bad word.'

As one, Aria and Enzo turned to the door. Mister Babbit had just popped his ears round. His head appeared next.

'Hello-o!'

Enzo used the opportunity to vent his frustration.

'Get out, Simple, and stop spying! I'll complain to Kleber!'

Simple appeared in the doorway.

'You've been slapped, you have. Serves you right.'

Aria stood up, rubbing her hand. She had hurt herself.

'Simple, you mustn't tell anyone what's just happened,' she said.

'Is it a secret?'

'A sort of secret.'

'Mister Babbit's got secrets too. Love secrets.'

'We've had enough of your randy rabbit!' Enzo shouted, coming over to him. 'Why the hell did we have to end up with a moron in the house?'

'Enzo, don't!' Aria ordered, thumping his shoulder.

Simple crushed Mister Babbit between his hands.

'Mustn't argue, mustn't argue,' he begged.

Then he took Aria by the arm and pushed her towards Enzo.

'Give him a kiss.'

Enzo and Aria looked at each other, Enzo shyly, Aria with an amused smile.

'A kiss. To make it better.'

Enzo half turned his head, presenting his enflamed cheek to Aria. And she kissed it.

'It's a good start,' Mr Villededieu reckoned.

'Really? Would you say?'

Enzo had gone downstairs to his old neighbour. He had a purple swelling over his cheekbone.

'Offending a woman gives you a hold over her, a right.'

Enzo looked at Mr Villededieu quizzically.

'The right to earn forgiveness. Give her some flowers with a little note in the middle. *What sweeter pain than to suffer by your hand* . . . the usual nonsense.'

Enzo shook his head slowly.

'I'm not feeling it.'

'Red roses. Ardent passion in the language of flowers. Or white ones. Virginal love. Except, in your case, it doesn't have to be.'

Enzo bought eleven pink roses. Then scribbled on a piece of card: *I'm so, so sorry.* He thought, *If I were a girl, it would break my heart seeing a boy grovelling like that.*

Aria went out to post a letter. Enzo slipped into her bedroom and put the flowers on her pillow. Then he went back to his room and lay down on his bed to wait.

'Are you fucking stupid or what?'

Enzo sat up and took the bouquet full in the face.

'Do you want Emmanuel to pulverise you?'

139

'No I . . . No, Aria . . .'

'Do this again, and I'll make you eat your flipping flowers.'

Mr Villededieu didn't want to appear out of his depth.

'She's protecting you from Emmanuel. That's a good sign.'

'George, I don't think you know anything about girls today. Flowers and coming on strong don't work any more. They're independent, they choose their man and they chuck him away like a used tissue when they're done with him. It's really tough being a man now. It's all explained in *Marie-Claire*.'

'The war of the sexes,' Mr Villededieu muttered. 'It's as old as time itself . . .' But he seemed to be bowing beneath the weight of all that time.

'You must be at least twenty years older than your wife, aren't you?' Enzo ventured suddenly.

George straightened. 'Twenty-two.'

'So how did you get her? With flowers or by being rough?'

'She married me for my money,' George admitted.

* * *

That Sunday morning, Corentin was the first to get up. Simple was awake too but Corentin never showed much interest in the resident idiot. As usual, he waited for Enzo to emerge before making any plans. He automatically looked at his watch.

'You're waiting for Enzo,' said Simple.

Corentin didn't bother replying.

'You're always waiting for Enzo.'

'What? No, I'm not, not always.'

He flashed Simple a furious look and repeated, 'Not always.'

Yet again, a nugget of truth had been revealed to him: he was always waiting for Enzo. Only the day before he had suggested they go to the swimming pool. He wanted to take some exercise to lose weight. Enzo had refused with the excuse that girls would just throw themselves at him if they saw him in his trunks. So Corentin had given up on the idea.

'Morning! You sleep well?'

Kleber had just come into the kitchen.

'Would you like to go to the pool this morning?' asked Corentin.

'Yeah, I'll get my rubber ring!' cried Simple.

*   *   *

The three of them went to the famous glass-roofed Piscine Pontoise. Kleber couldn't persuade his brother to use a float suit instead of his dolphin rubber ring. Simple was adamant: floats can't swim, dolphins can. As soon as he reached the smaller pool he jumped in with a huge splash, and squealed because the water was cold. Kleber glanced round quickly. There were a few outraged-looking mothers on the edge of the pool.

'He has learning difficulties,' he called out to them.

Without waiting for their reaction, he went and dived into the big pool. Simple, clinging to his rubber ring, was quick to join him. Simple was oddly put together; there seemed to be no substance to him – narrow shoulders, a hollow stomach and thin hips. Like a child on a larger scale.

On the last rung of the ladder, he made a point of enquiring of another bather: 'There isn't any sharks in the middle, is there?'

The only reply he got was a laugh.

'That man's mad,' Simple said under his breath.

Then he thought that sharks definitely wouldn't attack dolphins, seeing as they were practically the same family, and he swam away from the edge in his splashy breaststroke.

'You OK?' asked his brother, finishing his second length of crawl.

'I'm OK. I've done a wee.'

'What? Oh, not in the water I hope?'

'Yes.'

He looked pleased with himself.

'Get out. Hurry up!' Kleber scolded. 'Go on, quick!'

'Are there sharks?'

'Yes, get out.'

Kleber looked around for Corentin. He was holding on to the side catching his breath.

'Come on,' he called to him. 'We're going.'

'What? But I've still got twenty lengths to do!'

'We're leaving.'

Back outside on the pavement, Corentin was furious.

'God, can't you ever do anything normal?'

Kleber was walking alongside him, head lowered.

'I'm not going there again,' said Simple. 'There's too many sharks.'

Chapter 8

*Where Mister Babbit gives
pink roses to Zahra*

Zahra didn't know how to tell Kleber she loved him. At Corentin's birthday party, the only thing she could think to do was try and calm her feelings. 'Respect yourself and you'll be respected,' was one of her father's favourite expressions.

Right now, Zahra was wondering how to get Kleber to respect her a little less. But who could she get advice from? Zahra was the eldest of seven girls, and the prettiest – the jewel in their mother Yasmine's crown. But the favourite was Amira, the youngest, who was born deaf mute.

'All these girls,' grumbled Mr Larbi.

He adored them. But for the last few days he had been worried about Zahra. He had noticed she hardly laughed any more. 'When a girl is sad, look for the boy,' the saying went.

'Have you all remembered that Zahra's going to be seventeen next month?' he said as they had supper.

'How could we forget!' cried Djemilah, Leila, Naima, Nouria and Malika.

Amira said nothing but gave a beautiful smile. She had lip-read what her father said.

'Right, listen. "The pleasures of this world are but an illusion."'

'Oh, don't start that again,' protested Djemilah, who was fourteen and insolent with it.

'But it's in the Koran,' he said, put out. 'If you ever want to find the "Gardens of paradise" –'

'Allah's paradise is only cool for men,' Djemilah interrupted him again.

All the girls started laughing, except for Amira, who didn't understand.

'Oh, why couldn't you be the one who can't speak?' he sighed. 'In my day, when my father spoke, no one cut in. He used to say, "To listen is to obey."'

'In that case, I'd be very happy to be deaf,' said Djemilah.

Zahra, who had always been obedient, shot a frightened look at her sister.

Feeling powerless, Mr Larbi turned to his wife. 'But it's in the Koran . . .'

Their mother raised her hands and looked up to the heavens, a gesture that had no precise meaning but successfully kept her out of the dispute.

That evening Zahra ended up in her bedroom without having found anyone to talk to. She was trying to revise her chemistry, but pictures kept dancing before her eyes: Beatrice tantalising Kleber, Beatrice coiling up her hair, Beatrice walking away with Kleber.

'Is everything OK?'

Zahra slowly turned her grey-green eyes to Djemilah.

'Yeah, fine.'

The younger girl sat down next to her impatiently, pushing her slightly.

'Right, what's his name?'

'Kleber.'

'Funny name. Is he good-looking, at least?'

'Out of my league.'

'Haven't you looked at yourself? You're a star!'

Zahra smiled sadly.

'Does he like you?'

'At first I thought he did. But he's going out with someone else.'

'Is she pretty?'

Djemilah had a simplistic view of human relationships.

'She's a redhead with really hairy armpits. And she smells of pork.'

Pure fantasy but it made her feel better.

'You just have to reel him in,' whispered Dejmilah. 'Nothing difficult about reeling boys in.'

Zahra shuddered.

'Come here, come and have a look at yourself,' Djemilah said, dragging her sister to the mirror. She opened a couple of buttons on her top, hitched up her skirt, put some eyeliner round her eyes to make them sparkle, and showed her how to adopt a sultry expression with her lips half open and smouldering eyes.

'What are you up to?' asked Leila.

The three of them shared a bedroom.

'Playing harems!' replied Dejmilah.

Leila was only twelve but not exactly a late developer.

'I've got a strawberry-flavoured lipgloss,' she said, rummaging through her pencil case. 'It makes your lips look wet and makes your kisses all perfumy.'

'Have you been kissed already?' asked Zahra, horrified.

'Well, doh, what's life for?'

Soon the three of them were knotting their blouses above their navels, and dreaming about piercings and tattoos and hair braids.

'My legs are so hairy, they're rank,' wailed Dejmilah.

Leila went to nick their dad's razor and their mum's breast-firming cream. They then held a beauty contest and Zahra came out as the winner, without arousing any jealousy. In the end – massaged, made-up and half naked – Zahra lay on her bed, posing like the Sultan's favourite.

'If Kleber could see you now,' sighed Djemilah.

Not only did Kleber not see her then, but he didn't see her the following morning either. He stayed in his room, his brief trip to the swimming pool having produced a bout of bronchitis.

'Mister Babbit's coughing too. Ahem, ahem, ahem.'

The rabbit coughed away, bent double and flicking his ears in the air.

'Can't you leave me in peace?' begged Kleber, coughing, blowing his nose, eyes streaming.

Simple wandered about the room for a while, bored and sulky. Then he picked Mister Babbit up in one hand, his bag of Playmobil in the other, and clamped the girl rabbit between his teeth. This was his new obsession, carrying Babbita in his mouth.

'Can you stop that?' scolded Kleber. 'You're ruining her.'

'Ish jusht a toy.'

He went off to play in the living room. Just then, someone rang the doorbell. Simple, who had been trained by the other flatmates, pressed the button and ran to warn his brother.

'Ish Jahra.'

'What?'

'Ish Jahra.'

'Put that stupid toy down!'

When Kleber gathered that Zahra had come to bring him his homework, he was thrown in a panic. His hair was all greasy, his face kind of yellow and his eyes red.

'She mustn't see me,' he told Simple. 'Ask her to leave the work and say thanks from me.'

Zahra was disappointed not to see Kleber, but she would have been embarrassed going into his bedroom.

'Has he got flu?'

Simple shook his head and, speaking like a specialist, said, 'He has the coughing disease.'

Zahra smiled. She loved children and Simple was a child, after all.

'Have you got some work for Kleber?' he asked.

Zahra took her files out.

'Are there letters?'

Zahra started laughing.

'Yes. And numbers too.'

Simple nodded knowingly.

'12?'

'Can you count?' she asked, gradually giving in to her laughter.

'Yes. 1, 2, 3, 4, B, 12.'

Zahra was really laughing now. She tried to control it for fear of upsetting Simple, but the more she tried to calm herself, the more her laugh exploded out of her. Simple watched her, intrigued.

'You like laughing,' he pointed out.

Zahra wiped her eyes, laughter still bubbling in her throat. She put her hand on Simple's arm.

'Thanks. That did me good.'

When Zahra had left, Simple leafed through her files. She kept them very tidy but Simple inspected them with a critical eye.

'It's not very pretty.'

'Have you got a colouring pencil?' Mister Babbit suggested.

Simple went to get his pencil-case and made various attempts at writing in the physics file, choosing warm tones: red, yellow and orange. He decorated the history file with geometrical friezes in a series of blues from sky to navy, and the odd bit of purple and mauve. Then he practised the letter B in the maths file, eliciting a good many Babbitesque comments.

'That one's going to fall over. Oh no, the last one's got three tummies.'

Half an hour later, tired by his exploits, he pushed the file away and realised he had done something terrible. As he always did in these situations, he behaved as if this was some global catastrophe and wailed, 'Kleber!'

He ran into the bedroom, where his brother had finally managed to fall asleep.

'Kleber! I've done some scribbles!'

'Hey? What?'

Kleber raised an eyelid and got an avalanche of files in his face.

'I'm a naughty boy!' bawled Simple.

Emerging from his groggy state, Kleber leafed through the files.

'Please say you didn't do this? Oh my God, you did!'

He had just stumbled on one of the more elaborate friezes in the history file.

'Are you going to lose me in the woods?'

Kleber thought, *I'm going to take you back to Malicroix.* He couldn't handle his brother any more.

As if by fate, that same evening Mr Maluri rang his son. He was so wrapped up with his marriage to young Mathilda that he hardly ever called his boys.

'Everything OK?' he said. 'Are you coping with Simple?'

'It's hard. He does stupid things the whole time.'

'Well, I warned you about that.'

There was a pause. Kleber hoped for a helpful word, some compassion, a bit of advice.

'I don't know if they've still got room at Malicroix,' Mr Maluri said eventually.

'No, I don't necessarily mean that,' Kleber struggled. 'It's just I'm ill at the moment . . .'

A coughing fit illustrated the point.

'If you could have Simple this weekend . . .'

'Oh, no way, absolutely not.'

Mr Maluri realised how harsh this refusal sounded, and added, 'You see, Mathilda's pregnant. Simple frightens her. We don't know why he's abnormal.'

'But it was the pills Mum –' Kleber said feebly before succumbing to more coughing.

Mr Maluri let his son cough without interrupting him.

'So I just have to sort myself out, is that it?' Kleber eventually managed to whisper.

'I'll let social services know.'

Kleber hung up, shattered. But he was destined to get no rest that evening – Enzo knocked on his door. Kleber unburdened all his worries to him.

'What am I going to do about Zahra?'

'Roses,' said Enzo.

'Roses?'

'Give her roses. I've got some stunners – second-hand pink ones, good as new. And you put a card in the middle. *I'm so, so sorry.* I've even got the card if you want.'

When the others heard about Kleber's latest problem, they showed their solidarity. Corentin found some paper to wrap the bouquet, and Aria suggested Simple should do a drawing for Zahra.

'To say you're sorry. Good idea?'

'I'll draw Mister Babbit!'

Simple drew an irresistible rabbit with unbelievably expressive ears.

'But the man's a genius!' said Enzo ecstatically.

Simple was given a pad of drawing paper. Aria remembered seeing some remarkable drawings done by schizophrenics.

'Yes, you do get "idiots savants",' confirmed Emmanuel.

Kleber believed in his brother's talents and encouraged him to draw. Simple drew Mister Babbit at the party, at Mass, at the swimming pool, the supermarket . . .

'Maybe you could draw something different, not

154

just a rabbit?' suggested his brother after the twelfth portrait.

Simple shook his head.

'I only know how to do Mister Babbit.'

'Obviously that's a limiting factor,' said Corentin.

When Zahra arrived home from dropping off her files with Kleber, her sisters Leila and Djemilah wanted to know if she had seen her beloved.

'No, he was in his room.'

'Well, you should have gone in!' cried Leila, beside herself. 'You'd have seen him in bed.'

'Oh yeah, right,' Djemilah snarled at her younger sister. 'Kind of obvious you're only twelve.'

'Yes, all right, Granny!' said Leila, storming out.

'She's way too advanced for her age,' said Zahra.

Djemilah winked at her. 'She's right, though. You've got to go into his room. With a bit of luck,' she added, crossing her fingers, 'he'll still be there tomorrow.'

Djemilah was big on talk, but cautious in practice. She would go with her sister to avoid any risks. Zahra pretended to be scared of the whole idea . . . but not for too long, so as not to discourage Djemilah. All that remained was to establish the details of the plan, in other words: what to wear.

'I can't wear anything too sexy,' said Zahra. 'I'll be coming straight from college.'

They found the answer: a slinky strappy top under her blouse. As for Djemilah, she would wear a chador. At first Zahra protested, their mother was the only member of their family who wore one.

'No, really,' Djemilah insisted. 'He'll behave himself then.'

Then they agreed where to meet before heading for the Rue du Cardinal-Lemoine together.

The following afternoon they met at five o'clock and made their final preparations under a shop awning. Djemilah, who was wearing an ankle-length raincoat, knotted her scarf. Meanwhile, Zahra, under the cover of her jacket, unbuttoned her blouse, working up quite a sweat.

'Fab when you lean over,' said Djemilah. 'He's gonna go crazy.'

'You're the one who's crazy.'

When Zahra rang the entry-phone, Djemilah squeezed her arm to show her support. But she was in such a nervous state herself that she made her sister cry out in pain.

156

'Who is it?' said a voice. 'Hello, Mr Somebody? I'm very well, thank you.'

'Hello, Simple! Can you open the door?'

Simple ran to warn his brother. 'Kleber! Help!'

'What is it now?'

'It's Zahra. She's going to tell off me.'

'Get the flowers. Quick! Say you're sorry. And give her the files back. And remember your picture!'

Simple ran to the door and, in his panic, he dumped the flowers, the files and the pictures in Zahra's arms all in a heap.

'Mister Babbit did the scribbling. And I did the picture of Mister Babbit cos Kleber's going to lose me in the woods if I do it again.'

The sisters listened to him, not understanding a word but already succumbing to uncontrollable laughter.

'Oh bless, look at the rabbit's face!' said Djemilah.

'I did that, I did,' Simple preened. 'It's cos I'm a genius.'

The laughter grew louder. But Djemilah whispered to her sister, 'Are we going to his room, then?'

And the laughing stopped.

'Is Kleber here?' asked Zahra.

Simple nodded.

'I need to explain something to him for college.'

'Can you show us which is his room?' Djemilah added.

Zahra was hampered by the bouquet so she put it down on the dining-room table. Her sister murmured, 'Don't forget to lean over.'

Simple took the two girls to the end of the corridor.

Kleber had just had a coughing fit that made him feel hot all over, so he had pushed back his duvet. Simple came in without any warning.

'Uh-oh, he's got nothing on.'

The two girls were right behind him. Kleber, speechless, watched them come in, then bent forward to snatch the duvet and pull it back up. There was a rather muddled exchange of apologies.

'Look, I don't want to disturb you,' stammered Zahra, 'but I just wanted to warn you that we've got a . . . a . . . um . . .'

She couldn't remember.

'A book,' prompted Djemilah.

'There's this book we've got to read for philosophy. I've made a note of the references for you.'

She came over to the bed, leant forward and put a piece of paper down in front of Kleber. But the boy didn't take as much advantage of the view as he should have done, because he was terrified by Djemilah.

'Is this your sister?' he asked shyly.

'Yes,' said Djemilah. 'But I'm more traditional than Zahra. It's what I've chosen.'

Kleber gave a respectful nod. He really couldn't wait for the pair of them to leave.

'By the way, thanks for the flowers, but you really shouldn't have,' said Zahra, trying out one of the sultry expressions she had perfected with her sister.

'Yeah, I'm really sorry about my brother's scribbles.'

'What scribbles?'

Kleber blushed. So it was down to him to confess what his brother had done. Zahra flicked through her physics file. She was pretty put out. Meanwhile, Djemilah maintained a glum expression but didn't miss a single detail: the feverish Kleber, stripped to the waist, had quite an effect on her, every inch of her.

'It doesn't matter,' Zahra said eventually. 'I'll copy it out again. Right then, see you.'

Kleber had started coughing again. He gave a little wave, then buried his head in his pillow, embarrassed, ashamed and annoyed.

Back outside the apartment, Djemilah was the more excited of the two sisters.

'I hope you got to see everything you wanted,' she said.

Zahra elbowed her sister in the ribs. Then they hurtled down the stairs, screeching with laughter.

Chapter 9

Where Mister Babbit meets Mrs So-Shull

That Tuesday, Aria went out after lunch; she didn't want to be alone with Enzo again. Meanwhile, he had gathered that, without making an official arrangement, all the others had taken to landing him with the idiot when Kleber wasn't there.

'Simple?'

He was in his room, dressed very elegantly, complete with a tie.

'What the hell are you up to?' asked Enzo.

'Nothing.'

He was dressed up as a daddy. Mister Babbit was his son and Babbita his daughter. That was the game.

'I'm going out for a bit,' said Enzo. 'You be good, OK?'

'I'm Mr Mutchbinguen.'

Enzo glanced at him rather anxiously and repeated, 'Mutchbinguen?'

Simple confirmed it with a nod and added, 'I've got a son and I've got a daughter.'

'Brilliant. You bring them up well. I'll be back in an hour.'

An hour without a minder! Mister Babbit couldn't believe his ears. When the front door shut, his brain started boiling over.

'How about going everywhere?'

They started with Corentin's bedroom, where Mr Mutchbinguen had the satisfaction of finding a mobile phone. Simple pocketed it without a word. Then he went to Enzo's room.

'The exercise book!' Mister Babbit enthused.

The large exercise book with the small squared paper was on the bed.

'Mr Mutchbinguen writes stories,' said Mister Babbit.

Simple agreed with a magisterial nod of the head, and left the room with the book under his arm. He hesitated outside Aria and Emmanuel's room.

'Do you think the lil'men have left?'

Mister Babbit clearly remembered the strange noises produced early in the mornings. But he had an

162

answer for everything: 'The lil'men are frightened of Mr Mutchbinguen.'

Simple went into the bedroom with an air of great confidence.

'A tevelision!' he cried, seeing a computer screen lit up.

He came closer and saw the keyboard.

'It's a contuper,' he corrected himself.

He put Enzo's book on the desk and sat down.

'I'm going to do a bit of contuper.'

Emmanuel, who had been typing up notes from lectures, hadn't closed the document, and Simple made a few additions by clattering away on the keyboard. After clicking on a variety of icons, he looked at the screen. It seemed to be asking itself what was going on.

Simple remembered what you had to say in this sort of situation: 'Fuck, it's crashed!'

Mister Babbit laughed out loud. 'He says bad words, Mr Mutchbinguen does.'

Just then, Simple strained his ears and said, 'Shh.' He thought he had heard the entry-phone. Yes, there it was again.

*   *   *

'Hello, it's Mrs Bardoux from social services.'

Through the crackle of the intercom, all Simple picked up was 'Hello . . . it's Mrs . . . So-Shull.'

Simple pressed the button and waited for Mrs So-Shull out on the landing. She came up the stairs, with one hand to her chest, puffing.

'I don't . . . like lifts . . . This is Mr . . . Maluri, isn't it?'

'It's Mr Mutchbinguen,' Simple introduced himself.

'There are several tenants, aren't there?'

'There's the flatmates,' said Simple, stepping aside to let in the woman with the substantial backside.

'I see you're having a tidy up,' she said, pointing to the rabbit in Simple's hand.

'My son.'

'Mine had a manky old toy like that too. But, you're very young to be a father!'

'I've got a daughter too,' added Simple, delighted to have found someone to play with.

'Congratulations . . . Um, is Mr Maluri in?'

The mobile started vibrating in Simple's pocket. Startled, he murmured, 'The tephelone.'

'Hello, darling?' said a voice from the phone. 'It's Mum.'

Simple froze in astonishment. Mum was dead. But maybe when you died you became a lil'man?

'Hello, can you hear me, my bunny rabbit?'

'Yesss!' cried Simple, waggling Mister Babbit's ears.

'How are you?'

'It's a lovely day.'

'You sound odd on the mobile . . .'

Mrs Bardoux stepped aside to avoid intruding, and glanced round the living room.

'Listen,' Corentin's mother went on, 'we're thinking of coming to see you on Saturday.'

Aria and Corentin's parents, Mr and Mrs Mouchaboeuf, lived in Paimpol and didn't come to see their children in Paris very often. Their son and daughter had not thought it vital to let them know that one of the new flatmates had learning difficulties.

'Could your father and I sleep in the living room?'

Simple was getting more and more confused. Why did his father need to sleep? He wanted to clarify the situation by explaining that he was Mr Mutchbinguen.

'It's not Simple . . .'

'Well, I can't see what's complicated about it! Just say if it's a nuisance . . .'

'Yes!' cried Simple, who had already had enough of the phone.

He switched it off and went back to play with Mrs So-Shull in the living room. She had grasped that Mr Mutchbinguen had been rather exasperated by his call, but affected a neutral expression.

'Is everything all right?' he said urbanely. 'It's a lovely day.'

'Yes . . . well, it's been quite chilly since yesterday. Could I speak to Mr Maluri?'

Simple shook his head.

'Oh? Is he out . . . Could I ask you to give him a message?'

Woah! The game was getting complicated. Simple frowned.

'I've been contacted about Mr Maluri's brother. Who . . . has learning difficulties.'

She had adopted a pained tone of voice so as not to appear judgemental.

'An i-di-ot,' corrected Simple.

'If you like,' Mrs Bardoux retorted coldly, finding this Mr Mutchbinguen more unpleasant by the minute.

'Apparently, this boy – he's an adult, in fact – is looked after by his brother, who's a minor. You must be aware of the situation?'

As the woman seemed irritated, Simple thought the time had come to blame Mister Babbit.

'It's not me, it's . . .'

'Of course I realise it's not your responsibility, Mr Mutchbinguen! I'm only trying to see how we can help Mr Maluri. Incidentally, I have his first name, Kleber, but I don't have his brother's.'

Simple said nothing.

'Don't you know the young man's name? Even though he lives here?!'

Simple thought this must be a guessing game.

'Corentin?'

'Corentin,' Mrs Bardoux repeated to help herself remember. 'So, basically, could you tell Mr Maluri that there would be a place for Corentin at Malicroix, at least during the week. And Corentin could come back here at the weekend. I think that would be the best possible solution, although I wouldn't call it ideal. Tell Mr Maluri to get in touch with social services. I'll leave you a phone number . . . He should ask for Mrs Bardoux.'

Simple pocketed the piece of paper and decided to end this boring game.

'I'm going to play with my son,' he said, indicating Mister Babbit.

'Oh, I'm so sorry . . . I didn't know he was waiting for you. Right, I'll leave you then.'

Simple bundled rather than escorted Mrs So-Shull to the door.

Some people really make it quite clear when you're disturbing them, thought Mrs Bardoux.

When Simple went back to his room to play, the telephone vibrated again.

'It's a bloody pain,' said Mister Babbit, already stressed by the mobile.

'Corentin?' said a man's voice on the phone.

'What?' grunted Simple.

'Don't you talk to me like that,' said Corentin's father. 'Your mother's just told me you were very rude to her. I can tell you I won't have it. I can cut off your allowance, you know!'

As retaliation, Simple cut off the call. Then, thoroughly displeased with his acquisition, he took the phone back to Corentin's room.

Aria arrived home before Enzo. The first thing she noticed in her bedroom was the blue computer screen.

'Fuck, it's crashed again,' she muttered, jerking the mouse around on the mat.

She was so abrupt that she knocked the exercise book with squared paper to the floor. As she picked it up, Aria thought she recognised it. Wasn't this the book that Enzo carted all over the apartment with him? She opened it and read: *Emma was fatally pretty.* The first sentence of Enzo's novel. Aria frowned. What was this book doing here? The answer was obvious: while Aria was out, Enzo had come and put it on the desk. At first she felt inclined to go and chuck it in his face, like the flowers. But she could always have a little peek at it and pretend she hadn't touched it. What would he know?

She started reading the first chapter. Despite the crossings-out, the writing was legible. Aria quickly realised that Emma was her clone. Annoying. There was a boy who loved her, a boy with slight learning difficulties, called Lorenzo. Amusing. Aria started following Emma and Lorenzo's story in her imagination. She couldn't put it down. She lay on the bed. Chapter 4, 5, 6 ... She wanted to know what happened. Aargh, the story stopped at an exciting bit, a turning point for the poor boy.

Aria buried her head in her pillow. So Enzo was writing a novel? And he had some talent. She felt like reading the first chapter again: *Emma was fatally pretty.* Time had been suspended by Enzo's writing. Aria came back to her senses when she heard Emmanuel's footsteps. She slid the book under her pillow.

'In bed already? Were you missing me?' Emmanuel joked as he came in.

'Look at your computer. It looks dead.'

Emmanuel rushed over to the keyboard, and Aria took the opportunity to slip the book under her jumper. She would give it back to Enzo without a word. But she didn't find him in the living room and when she knocked on his bedroom door, there was no reply. She went in, looked at the shambles of books and clothes on his bed, and lobbed the book on top.

One by one the others came home. First Kleber, then Enzo, then Corentin, all three of them unaware of what had happened in their absence.

'Here, this is for you,' said Simple, handing a piece of paper to his brother.

Kleber read the phone number.

'Where did you find this?'

'Mrs So-Shull gave it to me.'

'What, a lady came here?'

Simple nodded.

'And who did she come to see?'

'Mr Mutchbinguen.'

Kleber repeated the name.

'She must have got the wrong floor.'

He promised himself he would talk to the concierge about it. 'Mutchbinguen', it sounded German or something.

'I'm stample,' Simple announced suddenly.

'You're what?'

'I'm stample.'

Kleber's eyes bulged.

'What does that mean?'

'It means "I'm hungry". How about you, are you stample?'

Kleber opened his mouth to reply, but couldn't manage it. Sometimes Simple was so random.

'Did you buy any golden tillping?'

'Till . . . what the hell's that? Why are you talking like that?'

'It's another language,' Simple explained gently. 'I'm talking another language. Golden tillping is crusty bread.'

'No, really,' Kleber fought back. 'Just talk normally. You're a pain in the arse, that's enough.'

'Uh-oh, bad cronglement.'

Kleber sniggered. It would be best to let Simple get on with it. He'd give up eventually. But at the supper table he asked Emmanuel to pass him the golden tillping.

'The what?' said Emmanuel.

'It's crusty bread,' said Kleber glumly.

'Really? Where do you get that?' asked Corentin.

'In tillpingeries, I should think.'

They all seemed to be waiting for more information.

'Simple's inventing words, that's all. Speaking another language. It's nothing.'

'Fantastic!' exclaimed Enzo. 'Golden tillping!'

Aria looked at him furtively. She couldn't seem to look him squarely in the face any more. *Emma was fatally pretty.* The sentence kept dancing round her head. She wanted to ask, 'Does Emma sleep with Lorenzo in the end?'

'I'm going to speak another language too,' decided Enzo. 'Simple, could you pass the pallatress?'

'What's that?' asked Simple.

'I thought you spoke another language . . .'

172

'Yes, but not the same of you.'

'"Pallatress" is salad. Corentin, help yourself to some pallatress, then could you flond it to me?'

'OK,' said Corentin, 'but can you flond me the golden tillping.'

By the end of the meal, Corentin and Enzo were crying with laughter and Aria kept exploding, ramming her fist against her closed lips.

'All right, it's OK for a bit,' said Emmanuel. 'But it's fucking boring after a while.'

'Uh-oh, bad cronglement.'

Corentin went to bed in a brilliant mood. They really should take out a patent on Simple, the man was priceless. His mobile vibrated at about ten-thirty.

'Corentin, it's Mum. Don't hang up, darling. If there's something wrong, we need to talk about it.'

'What?'

'No, don't get angry. So there might be a girl living with you there? But that doesn't bother us, you know.'

Mrs Mouchaboeuf was prepared to accept anything. If her son told her he was setting up house with Enzo, she would accept it. She had already been in tears all evening.

'What girl?' asked Corentin irritably.

'No, no, don't shout! It doesn't matter. You've got your own private life, that's quite normal. But that's no excuse for hanging up on us.'

Corentin felt a chill pierce right through him. His mother was going mad.

'Is Dad at home?' he said slowly.

'Yes, well, no . . . look, you can tell me. If you think we should keep your father out of . . .'

Mr Mouchaboeuf was sitting directly opposite his wife, and they gave each other conspiratorial nods.

Corentin was thinking.

'What sort of medication are you on?' he asked eventually.

Mrs Mouchaboeuf shot a horrified look at her husband.

'What is it?' he whispered.

Corentin's mother held the receiver away from her mouth and muttered, 'He's talking about medication.'

Mr Mouchaboeuf couldn't take any more. He snatched the phone from his wife. 'Are you ill?'

Corentin suddenly felt his whole world had turned upside down. Were his parents really his parents? Since Simple had come into his life, nothing was like before. He'd stopped smoking, stopped pigging out, started taking exercise. Corentin wasn't Corentin any more. *Anyway, that might not be my name*, he thought, remembering the golden tillping. He switched off his phone and went to knock on Enzo's door.

'What's the matter?'

'I feel weird.'

He told him what had just happened.

'Hey, hang on,' said Enzo, 'your parents have got serious Alzheimer's.'

'Oh, OK,' said Corentin, reassured. 'It's not me, then!'

In the room next door, Aria's ears had pricked up. She could hear two voices in Enzo's room. Nothing interesting about that, just Corentin coming for a chat. But she couldn't help thinking about Enzo. *Emma was fatally pretty.* She fell asleep with these words.

The following morning, when Aria was on her way back from lectures, she spotted Enzo in the living room. He was sitting on the sofa, writing. She hesitated then popped her head round the door.

'Are you working?'

'No.'

He blushed, his heart was pounding. Even though he had decided to stop loving Aria and to sleep with Emma in two or three hundred pages.

'So, how does it end?' she said, nodding at the exercise book.

Enzo wasn't surprised to have been found out. After all, he cultivated the image of a writer looking for inspiration.

'I don't know yet.'

She sat down quite close to him.

'I've read it,' she admitted.

'Read what?'

'"*Emma was fatally pretty.*"'

Enzo look at her incredulously.

'You . . . took my book and read it?'

'Oh, it's OK, you don't have to act all innocent. I read it because you put it on my desk.'

'Me? I didn't do that!'

'Stop it, Enzo!'

'But, I swear . . .'

'Anyway, I think it's really good.'

Enzo forgot his protestations.

'Really?'

'Brilliant even. You have to finish it.'

The world was turning upside down. Aria was taking an interest in Enzo.

'You see, I thought you were a loser and a bad influence on Corentin . . .'

'I am a loser and a bad influence on Corentin,' Enzo confirmed. 'But I plosh you.'

'You wh—'

'I plosh you. It means "I love you" in another language.'

The surprise made Aria throw her head back laughing.

'You are silly.'

The tenderness in her voice sent a shiver through Enzo. He moved his hand closer to Aria's wrist and stroked it with the tips of his fingers.

'Aria, couldn't we . . .'

'No,' she said. 'Because of Emmanuel.'

'Because of Emmanuel,' Enzo repeated meekly.

He fell back against the sofa with his eyes raised to the ceiling, like a martyr in a classical painting. Aria felt a wave rising in the depths of her stomach, about to propel her into Enzo's arms. She leapt to her feet in a turmoil.

'OK, I'll let you get on with your writing.'

Enzo watched her run away.

'She's in love with you, my boy,' deduced Mr Villededieu.

Enzo had come to confide in him again.

'Do you think so? I can't believe it . . .'

He was full of hope and despair at the same time.

'Emmanuel's much better than me, isn't he?'

'True, he seems more of a man than you. But girls nowadays like boys.'

'George, you read too much *Marie-Claire*.'

'Your problem,' the elderly neighbour went on, 'isn't your rival. It's that little Aria. I'm sure she thinks it's very nice having a boyfriend *and* someone who loves her.'

Enzo nodded his head in silence.

'Make her jealous,' whispered Mr Villededieu.

An opportunity presented itself that evening. Having got hold of the apartment's telephone number, Mrs Bardoux decided to call Kleber at supper time. Enzo answered the phone.

'It's Mrs Bardoux. I would like to speak to Mr Maluri.'

'Oh, is that you, Stephanie? I didn't recognise your voice.'

'You must be thinking of someone else. I'm Françoise, Françoise Bardoux from social services.'

'This evening? Look, I can't, it's late already . . .'

'Could I speak to Mr Maluri?' bellowed Mrs Bardoux.

'Tomorrow? If you like, but don't meet me at my apartment.'

Aria listened in. A girl was coming on to Enzo. A student from the French department probably. *They've got nothing better to do*, thought Aria furiously. Meanwhile, Mrs Bardoux had hung up, leaving Enzo to talk to a dead line. 'OK, I'll come to your apartment. But I won't stay long, I'm knackered at the moment. OK, see you!'

He turned round, delighted with his acting talent, but was met by Aria's glowering eyes and immediately regretted what he had done.

'Who's this Stephanie, then?' asked Corentin.

'Oh, it's this poor girl. She's as ugly as . . . as a not very pretty thing.'

In his enthusiasm to quash Stephanie, Enzo had overdone it a bit. In Aria's imagination Stephanie now loomed like Miss World grafted on to a Bond girl.

* * *

179

As for Kleber, he was trying to find Mr Mutchbinguen to give him Mrs So-Shull's number.

'I haven't been in this building very long,' said the concierge, 'but I've never know a Mr Mutch-thingy. You should ask Mrs Villededieu. She's got family in Germany.'

Mr Villededieu was delighted to see the nice young man who went to Mass.

'Mutchbinguen?' he said pensively. 'Hey, Yvette, wasn't that your second husband's name?'

Mrs Villededieu shrugged. 'Oh, for goodness' sake! His name was Pompon. That's why I divorced him. Yvette Pompon! Mind you, now it's Villededieu, and that's not much better.'

Kleber took his leave of the couple.

'You'll just have to ring the number the woman left,' George suggested out on the landing.

Kleber felt stupid for not thinking of it sooner.

'Hello, can I help you?' said a tired voice.

'Um, hello, I'd like to speak to Mrs So-Shull please.'

'There's no one of that name here. Which service are you looking for?'

'Service? None . . . I'm not.'

Kleber hung up.

'Service,' he murmured.

Mrs So-Shull? Which Service?

'Social services . . .'

Uh-oh bad cronglements.

Chapter 10

*Where Mister Babbit makes friends
with the little deaf girl*

Kleber shared the hope, fairly widespread amongst the young, that problems sort themselves out if you avoid thinking about them. He decided to forget about Mrs So-Shull and Mr Mutchbinguen. He had other fish to fry.

Judging by his classmates' conversations, Kleber was convinced he was the only one who still hadn't slept with a girl. Which was all the more depressing because he knew that love would be the biggest thing in his life.

He thought about Beatrice the whole time. One day the only word she could utter was 'Kleber'. The next she almost seemed to have forgotten his name. She would suggest a trip to the cinema, then forget to confirm it. 'I'll call you'; she didn't call. He gave up expecting to hear from her; she called him.

Kleber needed to confide in someone, but the moment he said 'Beatrice' to Simple, his brother would go and find Babbita and smack her head against the wall. In desperation, he reread that great classic of French literature, *The Red and the Black*, which he had studied in the fifth form. How did Julien Sorel, shy and socially inferior as he was, go about nabbing Madame de Rênal? '*He was a young man of eighteen or nineteen, with irregular, though delicate features ... Large dark eyes which, in quiet moments, revealed reflection and fire ...*' If you added glasses to the portrait, it was the dead spit of Kleber. '*Julien put his mouth close to Madame de Rênal's ear and, at the risk of compromising her horribly, he said:*

"*Madame, tonight, at two in the morning, I shall come to your room, there is something I must tell you ...*"

Kleber went into Madame de Rênal's room deep in the night. '*A few hours later, when he emerged from Madame de Rênal's room, it could be said, as a novel would, that he no longer had anything to desire.*' Kleber sighed.

'What is it what you're doing?' asked Simple.

'Can't you tell? I'm being cultivated!'

Kleber had to try his luck like Julien Sorel. Beatrice had told him she was staying at home revising her maths this Saturday afternoon. He would drop by to offer to help. But what could he do with Simple while he was out? Enzo didn't want to take care of him any more. Kleber then had a rather underhand idea: he would leave his brother with Zahra.

'I need to buy some clothes,' he told the girl. 'But Simple is a nightmare in shops. Could I leave him with you for a couple of hours on Saturday?'

'I'll ask my mother.'

When their mother heard that Kleber had a brother with learning difficulties, she opened her heart and her front door wide to him.

That Saturday, Zahra, Djemilah, Leila and Malika were all there to greet the two brothers.

'Where's the boys?' asked Simple, having had a good look round.

The girls started laughing.

'There's only girls here,' Kleber told him, hopping

184

about on the doorstep as if warming up before a race.

'Girls are silly,' announced Simple. 'I don't want to stay, I don't.'

'I've got some colouring pencils,' said Zahra. 'Will you draw some rabbits for us?'

Kleber winked at her and slipped away. Simple was very annoyed. He pointed at Leila and Malika, saying, 'I'm not doing rabbits for hern or for hern.'

'Did you hear that, he says "hern" instead of "her",' laughed Malika with all the authority of a nine-year-old.

'That's cos I'm speaking another language!' cried Simple, annoyed.

'It's cos you're a spaz!'

'Well, you're a gozbongle!'

Hearing the row, their mother hurried to the door.

'Oh, is he here? Hello . . . Hello, how are you? I'm Yasmine. Come in, come in,' she said, speaking loudly, as if Simple were deaf.

Simple did as he was told, muttering, 'I don't like anyone here, I don't.'

He twirled Mister Babbit's ears in the depths of his pocket.

'How are we going to keep him busy?' asked their mother.

'I want to leave,' Simple said under his breath.

He stood in the middle of the living room, eyes lowered, down-turned mouth quivering. He couldn't understand why Kleber had abandoned him in this house full of girls. The sound of footsteps made him look up. Amira had come in. The little deaf-mute girl signed to her mother, making small guttural noises. Simple watched, amazed. Amira was ugly. She had had an operation on her eyes but she still had a slight squint and she wore glasses with very thick lenses. Her hearing aid, which made her ears stick out, provided her with only a distant echo of the world. She smiled at Simple and waved him over.

'She's going to show you her toys,' said her mother.

Simple followed Amira, who shared a bedroom with Malika.

'Will you keep an eye on them?' their mother asked Malika.

The latter heaved a sigh. Keeping an eye on an idiot and a deaf girl, some weekend! Amira was opening a trunk and taking out her favourite dressing-up clothes, a princess dress, Aladdin's slippers, a fairy hat . . . all treasures that brought a twinkle to Simple's eyes.

'You go away,' he told Malika. 'I'm only playing with hern.'

He pointed at Amira.

'Well, that's fine by me,' said Malika, snapping the door shut angrily.

Next Amira opened her jewellery box. Mister Babbit couldn't keep quiet any longer. The tips of his ears peeped out. 'Hello-o!'

'Gold and diamonds! I'm rich, I'm rich!' he cried, launching himself at the jewels.

Amira burst out laughing.

Then Mister Babbit had a brilliant idea. 'We could be ladies!'

They found everything they needed in the chest: an old full-length skirt of Yasmine's shawls and scarves, a fan, a pink straw hat, an apron . . . Mister Babbit dressed as a farmer's wife with a red scarf over his ears, Amira put on the princess dress, and Simple pulled the long skirt over his trousers and covered himself in jewels.

'We could do our faces!' suggested Mister Babbit.

187

Amira went to the bathroom to fetch eyeliner, eye-shadows, lipsticks and blushers. Simple stood in front of the wardrobe mirror and made-up his eyes.

'I'm putting on some blue,' he said, plastering it over one eyelid. 'And a bit of . . .'

He looked at the palette of eyeshadows. 'Of poo.'

He spread a shimmering bronze on the other eyelid.

'Can you give me some lip-red?' Mister Babbit asked Amira.

The girl drew a pretty red heart on the rabbit's lips, then brought out his cheeks with a touch of blusher.

'You're beautiful, madam,' Simple complimented him.

'Yes, but I stink.'

Amira had a whole collection of perfume samples. They rubbed some on to Mister Babbit.

'You put some on your socks,' he told Simple. 'Your feet smell.'

The game was already fairly advanced when Zahra realised Malika wasn't watching Simple and Amira at all. She ran to the bedroom and found the pair of them covered in motley rags and daubed with make-up. It was such an extraordinary sight and Simple and

Amira looked so guilty that Zahra could barely suppress her laughter.

'It wasn't me,' said Simple. 'It was Mister Babbit.'

'Oh, poor thing!' she said, noticing the toy which had been smeared with a greasy red heart.

Zahra gradually assessed the extent of the disaster. The room reeked, and there were broken eye-shadows, squashed lipsticks and stained clothes.

'Amira, Amira!' she scolded, waving her hand at her little sister.

The child pointed an accusing finger at Mister Babbit. He was the one who wanted to play ladies.

Meanwhile, Kleber was playing at being a man.

'Really?' said Beatrice, finding him on her doorstep.

'Yes, I was in the neighbourhood . . . Could we do some maths revision together?'

'My parents'll be back soon,' said Beatrice with an ambiguous smile.

The message could be taken two ways. One, which was favourable to Kleber's advances, pointed out that Beatrice was alone. The other sounded like a warning. Alone, yes, but not for long.

'Do you want to see my bedroom?'

Kleber gave a simultaneous nod and shrug that meant 'Why not?'.

Beatrice's room looked like something from a doll's house, little pine bed, little lift-top desk, little shelf unit for ornaments. Kleber looked round and felt as if his feet were huge.

'How do you like it?'

'It's . . . it's . . .'

He pulled a non-committal face. He had pictured thick carpets and a vast bed with dark-coloured hangings on a canopy. Madame de Rênal's bedroom, gone midnight.

'I don't understand the exercises he's given us at all,' Beatrice said, picking up her maths file.

Kleber pressed up against her, shoulder to shoulder, and, still pretending to read the worksheet, put his arm round her waist.

'Hold on, are you here to work or to make out?'

He laughed mischievously.

'Can't we do both?'

Beatrice moved away slightly. She was growing wary of Kleber. He was getting more sure of himself.

'My parents are coming back.'

'You said that.'

He was smiling but didn't lose any time putting his hands where he wanted to.

'Hey, stop that, OK?'

'I love you,' he blurted.

He held her tightly to him. She struggled a bit, then let him kiss her. Kleber couldn't believe his luck. She was giving in, she really was! All at once, he felt *he* was being held tightly. She was pressing herself against his hips, rubbing up to him like a cat. How did Julien Sorel cope? The novel was not very explicit. He probably pushed Madame de Rênal back on to the bed. Kleber noted that Beatrice's bed was a bit of a long way away and quite small. He ran the risk of ending up sprawled on the carpet or of knocking Beatrice out against the wall. But, more importantly, he would soon be in a state where he no longer had anything to wish for, as a novel would say. He was the one who pushed Beatrice away. She lifted her hair off her neck. Phew. So hot suddenly. Then she started looking for a pen, a piece of paper, she opened her exercise book, closed it again. Seriously random.

'Right, well . . . I'll leave you to revise,' stammered Kleber.

He really couldn't leave like that. He had gained

some ground, he needed to indicate the fact, plant a little flag.

'You're not angry with me?' he breathed into Beatrice's neck.

'You're . . . annoying. It's all you can think about.'

But Kleber felt this was a flattering criticism. She had stopped seeing him as a little boy.

'I love you,' he said, his voice very masculine.

He didn't dare hug her again. Once more might be once too often. He left the apartment, fairly pleased with his progress, but aching as if he had done an hour's wrestling.

Down on the street, he breathed in . . . and out . . . in . . . and out. He took as much time as he needed to calm down before going back to Zahra.

'What did you buy?' she asked.

'Buy? Oh, yes, buy! Um, nothing. It was rubbish.'

She gave him a strange, piercing look. He blushed.

'How did things go with Simple?'

'He gets on brilliantly with Amira.'

When Kleber went into Amira's bedroom, Mister Babbit was just finishing his drying session with the hair dryer.

'The lip-red hasn't all gone,' Simple told his brother.

The rabbit now had a sort of bloodied smile.

'Not great,' Kleber muttered.

He thanked Zahra and her mother, then took Simple to the Tuileries Gardens, to watch children with their sailing boats. He felt like crying, but he didn't know why.

While Kleber and Simple were dawdling at the Tuileries, Aria and Emmanuel were working, her on the bed, him at the desk. From time to time, Aria listened out to hear whether Enzo was home.

'Did someone ring the bell?' asked Emmanuel.

As he stayed stuck to his chair, Aria got up with a sigh.

'Dad?' she said, seeing her father stepping out of the lift. 'Mum?'

Mr and Mrs Mouchaboeuf kissed their daughter with the sort of ceremony usually reserved for funerals.

'We tried to call you,' said Mr Mouchaboeuf, 'but we kept getting a Mr Mutchbinguen, who talked about the rain and what a nice day it was.'

'You must have dialled the wrong number,' replied Aria.

'No, darling, really not,' said Mrs Mouchaboeuf despondently. 'Your father and I think that Corentin's very unwell.'

Aria looked at them in astonishment.

'Oh, explain yourself better than that!' said Mr Mouchaboeuf irritably.

'Shhh, he may be here,' murmured his wife.

'No, he's gone out,' said Aria. 'But what's the matter with him?'

'He thinks he's called Mr Mutchbinguen.'

Aria's father explained that Corentin had taken to talking to them horribly abruptly on his mobile.

'When we tried to get you on the landline, he happened to pick up. He refused to let you know and he talked like a robot. Unrecognisable.'

Mrs Mouchaboeuf let out a sob. Aria thought her parents must have got hold of Simple. But they claimed Corentin had also spoken oddly on his mobile. That wasn't so easily explained.

'Haven't you noticed anything?' her mother asked.

At first, Aria shook her head, then she froze.

'What?'

'No, nothing . . . Corentin's stopped smoking, that's

all. And instead of putting on weight, which he normally does, he's lost some.'

'He's lost weight!' Mrs Mouchaboeuf repeated, hopelessly dismayed by the news.

'Has he lost a lot of weight?' asked Mr Mouchaboeuf, putting tragic emphasis on the 'lot'.

'Four or five kilos. But he looks good. He was a bit chubby . . . Sorry, someone's ringing.'

Aria pressed the entry-phone button as a voice announced, 'Mrs Bardoux.'

She was embarking on a new offensive. There was something suspect about the flatshare on the Rue du Cardinal-Lemoine. She was surprised to find three people huddled just inside the door.

'Hello,' she said rather tartly. 'Mrs Bardoux from social services. I'm here about Corentin's admission, I don't know if you've been told?'

'Oh my God!' Mrs Mouchaboeuf cried, clasping her hands together.

'What are you talking about?' asked Aria.

'I, um, could I ask your name please?' Mrs Bardoux replied, losing her patience. 'I don't need to give you any details of Corentin's case.'

'But we're his *parents*!' wailed Mrs Mouchaboeuf.

Just then, a key turned in the lock and Kleber came in, followed by his brother.

'There's too many people,' roared Simple, barging past everyone who was standing in his way.

'You certainly know how to use your elbows, Mr Mutchbinguen,' observed Mrs Bardoux in a pinched voice.

'I'm Simple.'

Mrs Bardoux wanted to score a point off him: 'There's a big difference between simple and downright rude!'

'Wait a minute, wait a minute!' cried Mr Mouchaboeuf. 'Why are you calling him Mr Mutchbinguen?'

'Because it's his name,' replied Mrs Bardoux.

Kleber eyed the woman more and more anxiously . . . and she noticed.

'You wouldn't by some remote chance be Mr Maluri, would you?' she asked, then gave a little cry of triumph and added, 'At last! And is Corentin with you?'

'No . . .'

'You mean you're not looking after him?'

'I can't see why I should look after Corentin,' Kleber replied, confused.

'I'm not criticising, you're very young,' said Mrs Bardoux, though her expression was stern. 'But this is still very irresponsible. Where is he?'

'Corentin? I, um . . . I haven't got a clue,' mumbled Kleber.

'Has he disappeared?' Mrs Mouchaboeuf panicked.

At that precise moment, another key turned in the lock. It could have been Enzo, it could have been . . .

'Corentin!' cried Aria, his father, his mother and Kleber.

He took a step back.

'Close the door,' Mrs Bardoux said authoritatively. 'He'll run like a rabbit . . .'

'Hello-o!' said a voice behind Mrs Bardoux's back.

She felt something resting gently on her shoulder. She turned her head slightly and jumped out of her skin. Two long ears had just brushed across her cheek. She ducked aside and glowered at Mr Mutchbinguen, who was waggling the cuddly toy.

'Who is it?' he asked cheekily.

'It's Mister Babbit!' yelled Corentin.

They're all mad, thought Mrs Bardoux.

*   *   *

As soon as Kleber had managed to establish that Simple was his brother with learning difficulties, everyone grasped that Mr Mutchbinguen was just something Simple had made up. Corentin's mother conceded that, because of his limitations, Simple had unwittingly upset her on the phone.

'Mind you,' she said to her son, 'it was you I spoke to on your mobile, wasn't it?'

Corentin stared intently at Simple.

'It wasn't me,' he said. 'It was Mister Babbit.'

Before leaving, Mrs Bardoux arranged to see Kleber the following Saturday.

'Try to come without your brother. It'll be easier to talk.'

Chapter 11

Where Mister Babbit heads back
to Malicroix

The following Saturday, Kleber dropped Simple at Zahra's again. Little Amira was waiting behind the door and jumped for joy when she saw her friend. Simple had a smile like a hammock hanging from ear to ear.

'They understand each other perfectly,' said Djemilah. 'I'm not sure how they do it.'

Amira tilted her head to one side and pointed at Simple's pocket. He shot his hand in and took out Mister Babbit.

'Hello-o!'

Kleber and Zahra caught each other's eye and smiled.

'I've got to go,' he said. 'My meeting's at two.'

*   *   *

Mrs Bardoux was waiting for Kleber in a small office lined with metal cupboards.

'Sit down, Mr Maluri. I'm glad you could get some time to yourself. What a life you lead!'

She looked at him with such compassion that Kleber even began to feel a bit sorry for himself.

'Well,' he said, 'it's not fun all the time.'

'You're a wonderful brother. Your devotion is way beyond what can be expected of someone so young . . .'

Kleber wondered whether social services were going to give him some sort of medal.

'But you should be thinking about yourself a bit too. You mustn't take this self-sacrifice so far that it threatens your own future.'

Having a brother with learning difficulties wasn't an asset for picking up girls, but Kleber didn't exactly feel threatened.

'I'm not advocating selfishness, of course, but we need to keep a sense of proportion in everything.'

Mrs Bardoux liked spewing out endless vacuous sentences. She took a good ten minutes to get to the point. 'Mr Maluri, I've been talking to your father. He's asked us to be good enough to reconsider the possibility of Simple, I mean Barnaby, being readmitted to Malicroix.'

Kleber, who was starting to nod off, jolted. 'Malicroix?'

'Yes, I know . . .' she said, putting up a hand to pre-empt any objections from Kleber. 'I know that you have formed a number of poor opinions concerning the establishment. But it is under new management now and, though some of their methods were open to criticism in the past, perhaps excessive medication for example, the staff have different instructions . . .'

And blah, blah, blah. Kleber felt sleep weighing his eyelids down again.

'Basically, what I'm suggesting, along with your father – who *is* Barnaby's legal guardian – is for him to be admitted there during the week, from Mondays to Fridays. You can go and pick your brother up on Friday evenings or Saturday mornings, the choice is yours. It's not that far on the train.'

A few weeks earlier, Kleber would have cried 'Malicroix, never!' But he was worn down. Mrs Bardoux's arguments seemed sensible, particularly as she dressed them up with so many compliments.

'Your father will come and pick Barnaby up on Sundays and drive him back to Malicroix,' Mrs Bardoux concluded.

Kleber shook her hand at the end of the meeting. Mister Babbit's fate was sealed.

'So what did she want from you then?' asked Zahra.

Kleber shrugged his shoulders as if it was no big deal. 'She suggested I should send Simple to Malicroix during the week.'

'And you said no?' Zahra asked as if it was obvious.

'No.'

Neither of them spoke for a moment, embarrassed.

'Simple has had fun with Amira,' Zahra said eventually. 'They had rabbit drawing competitions . . .'

Kleber felt angry, as if Zahra were accusing him of something.

That evening, while his brother was out of the room, Kleber told the others about the decision made by social services.

'Does Simple know?' asked Enzo.

'Not yet.'

'Can't you oppose it?'

'Well, my father's his . . . his legal guardian.'

Kleber was flooded with shame. He could have opposed it.

'I'll go and pick him up on Friday evenings. I'll look after him all weekend.'

His voice was shaky.

'It's better for your schoolwork,' Emmanuel comforted. 'You can't organise your life around your brother. And Simple needs his own space too. There are specialised teachers at Malicroix, they'll stimulate his intellect. He's vegetating here.'

Kleber thanked Emmanuel with a nod.

'Hey, hang on, that's a load of crap!' Enzo blurted. 'Haven't you ever heard Simple playing his Malicroix game? He's terrified of the place!'

Kleber hid his face in his hands.

'Oh, that's clever,' said Emmanuel, shooting a filthy look at Enzo. 'Do you think you're helping him?'

'I don't give a stuff about helping him! I'm thinking about Simple.'

'And you're going to look after him, are you? Didn't you say just the other day that you didn't want him dumped on you any more when Kleber was out?'

The two men were standing glowering at each other now.

'No need to tear each other to pieces,' Corentin intervened.

Aria put her hand on Enzo's arm to calm him. Emmanuel watched the gesture, his face taut with anger.

'What's the battle for?'

Everyone had thought Simple was in bed and his sudden appearance doused the atmosphere.

'It's nothing,' said Aria. 'The boys are arguing over nothing.'

'They want to send you back to Malicroix,' said Enzo.

Aria punched him on the shoulder.

'Stop saying the first thing that comes into your head like that!'

'Was it the first thing that came into my head or the truth?'

'I'm not going to Malicroix, am I?' Simple said, looking enquiringly at his brother.

'Not . . . not now,' mumbled Kleber.

'Later?'

'Yes.'

'In twelve years?'

'A . . . a bit less.'

'Next Monday,' Enzo said harshly.

He earned another punch.

'Mustn't hit Enzo,' said Simple.

Corentin couldn't swallow properly. He had never witnessed such a painful scene.

'Mister Babbit doesn't want to go to Malicroix, he doesn't.'

'You know he's just a cuddly toy,' said Aria.

Simple shook his head.

'He's going to throw himself out of the window.'

It was a suicide threat. Corentin snapped and left the living room to go and sob in peace in his own room.

Emmanuel went over to Kleber to say quietly, 'Don't let that influence you. There are always bars on the windows in places like that.'

That knocked the breath out of Kleber.

Aria took Simple by the hand and led him off down the corridor. Kleber heard her voice moving away: 'It's only for a few days, you know. Sometimes you'll be at Malicroix and sometimes you'll be here. It's so Kleber can do his schoolwork. You love your brother, don't you?'

Emmanuel gave Kleber a couple of comforting pats. 'You'll see, it'll be fine. There's got to be a balance between what's best for him and what's best for you.'

Enzo turned his back on them and went to look out of the window. They had each chosen their camp.

The next few days went by without a hitch. Kleber spoke to Simple about Malicroix. He showed him a calendar and put a cross against each day from Monday to Friday.

'On Saturdays and Sunday you'll come back here and we can go for walks in the Tuileries Gardens, and . . .'

'And go to see Amira?'

'And go to see Amira,' Kleber confirmed.

Enzo had been right. Simple had to be told the truth, and in simple terms. But, since the confrontation, Enzo had kept away from the apartment as much as possible. He took refuge at the Sorbonne's library, where he sat writing his novel. When he thought of Aria, he rubbed his shoulder. In the next few chapters, Emma had a seriously hard time.

At college Kleber avoided Zahra.

'It's a pain you've got your brother at the weekend, though,' Beatrice saw fit to tell him. 'Doesn't solve any problems for going out. And stuff.'

Kleber thought that, if he could get Simple to agree to spending some weekends at Malicroix, he might find out what "stuff" was.

That Sunday, Kleber had to pack his brother's suitcase. Everything posed a problem. Should he put the Playmobil things in? And the Heroes? And the vevolver? What clothes apart from trackies? Simple wasn't going to be allowed to dress up as Mr Mutchbinguen. Kleber stood in the middle of the room, his arms hanging limply by his side.

He started with sweatshirts and picked up a pile of them from the wardrobe. That was where he found Corentin's lighters. He felt oddly relieved. It was proof that Simple was potentially dangerous. Now he had an answer to his misgivings. He filled a big bag with toys and folded Simple's suit.

'Are you going on a journey,' asked Simple, coming into the room.

'No, but you are. I told you . . .'

Simple's face dropped. 'It's not today, is it?'

'Yes. Look, I've put your toys in the suitcase.'

'Is that mine own suitcase?'

Simple seemed flattered. He picked it up by the handle and admired himself in the mirror.

'Mr Mutchbinguen's going on a journey, he is . . . he's going to . . . to . . .'

His panic was making him breathless.

'To Marjabodger,' he said in one big breath. 'That's the other language.'

Right then Kleber wished he did speak another language and live in another place.

Mr Maluri arrived at the end of the evening. He hadn't seen his sons for more than two months.

'This is Daddy,' Simple told Kleber, as if he felt introductions were needed.

Mr Maluri hugged his boys.

'I won't be able to do this every weekend,' he warned. 'Mathilda's seven months gone . . . Right, is that his suitcase?'

'Yes,' said Kleber, 'but I was just thinking . . .'

'You weren't thinking anything. You've already done too much thinking. And you can see where it's got us. Right back to square one. And if you'd gone on much longer there wouldn't have been any room at . . . at Thingy.'

'Nah, nah, nah, nah,' Simple imitated him in a scolding tone.

Mr Maluri looked slightly put out. But then he grabbed the suitcase, keen to get this chore over and done with. Kleber saw his brother down to the street.

'That's Daddy's car,' said Simple. 'Daddy's putting the case in the boot. He's opening the door. He's got the key, he has.'

Under his breath, he gave a running commentary of his father's every move as if it was a succession of great exploits. Kleber watched out of the corner of his eye. He was worried there could be a scene at the last minute.

'Can I go in the front?' asked Simple.

'Yes, but don't touch anything,' said Mr Maluri gruffly.

Simple looked pleased.

'OK, see you on Friday,' said Kleber. 'I'll come and pick you up, you do understand, don't you?'

'I'm going in the front,' Simple replied as if nothing was more important than that.

He didn't give his brother a hug but sat himself down on the passenger seat.

'Don't start fiddling with everything!' grumbled Mr Maluri. 'Right, I'm off. You'll be OK on Friday?'

He was talking to Kleber while apparently very preoccupied with adjusting his wing-mirror.

'It'll be fine,' said Kleber.

And his father set off without a backward glance. As soon as they had shut the door of the apartment, a grim silence descended.

Supper was a gloomy affair.

'Poor old Simple,' said Corentin, 'the place did have a good feel to it with him around.'

Enzo stood up almost before he sat down, took an apple and some bread and slipped back to his room. They were all in their rooms early.

'Corentin's right,' Emmanuel said to Aria. 'The place doesn't feel the same. Why don't we leave?'

'Leave? Where would we go?'

'Well, we could rent a studio. Just the two of us.'

Emmanuel had been thinking about this for a while, but Aria hadn't been expecting it at all. She thought she could easily talk him out of the idea.

'We can't afford it.'

'My parents will help me.'

'Do you think?'

Emmanuel tried to sound casual. 'Yes, if I tell them we're getting married.'

Aria jumped as if she'd been given an electric shock, but hid her feelings behind a little laugh.

'Whoa, where did that come from? It's a bit soon, don't you think?'

'I'm twenty-five. I love you.'

He looked at her questioningly.

'I love you too. But I . . . I want to finish my course first. And I need to think about Corentin . . .'

Emmanuel resisted the urge to bellow 'And Enzo!'

'Yes, of course. Anyway, I don't expect an answer straight away. Will you think about it?'

'Yes,' Aria whispered and snuggled up to him. But just as she was falling asleep, a collection of words floated before her closed eyes and lined themselves up: *Emma was fatally pretty.*

On Monday, Kleber felt free as a bird that had flown its cage. On Tuesday, he was still savouring his freedom. On Wednesday, he called Beatrice. He wanted to persuade her to drop by the apartment. She put up some resistance. He laughed and grew irritable. 'OK, I'm going to hang up,' Beatrice threatened. They spent most of the afternoon like this. On Thursday, Kleber felt really depressed. He wanted to call his father for news of Simple. What did he do when they got to Malicroix? He remembered Simple carrying his suitcase and admiring himself in the mirror. His eyes welled with tears. Simple had been playing a part, the part of Mr Mutchbinguen.

'Dad? It's Kleber. I just wanted to know . . . have you had any news of Simple?'

'You're seeing him tomorrow, aren't you?'

'Yes, but did everything go OK on Sunday?'

There was a pause on the other end.

'Dad?'

'Yes, yes, I'm here. What do you want me say? He made a hell of a scene!'

Kleber felt his legs giving way. He sat down.

'Really?'

'Of course!' Mr Maluri said irritably. 'The staff at Malicroix explained it all. He wasn't used to it any more. He'll have to re-adapt to the place. If you hadn't had your hare-brained scheme . . .'

'What did he do?'

'He caused a scene, like I said!' he cried. 'Lashing out, trying to escape. It took several of them to hold him.'

Kleber couldn't listen to any more.

Friday was horrible. The hours went too quickly and too slowly. Kleber couldn't wait to free his brother, but he was afraid of facing him. At the end of lessons he didn't wait for Beatrice but ran to catch up with Zahra, who had been the first to leave.

'Zahra!'

She turned round.

'Zahra,' he said again.

He had been avoiding her all week, making it so clear that he was with Beatrice that everyone else started calling them 'Mr and Mrs Maluri'.

'I'm going to pick Simple up later.'

'Do you want us to have him on Saturday?' Zahra said flatly.

'Yes, no, wait. Can we walk together?'

They walked on in silence. But Zahra knew all about hearing what someone was saying when they weren't talking.

'How are things with your brother?'

'Not good.'

He squeezed her wrist. He didn't know what he was doing.

'I'm worried about going there on my own.'

Zahra got it. He needed her.

'Would you come with me?'

She could have said, 'Why don't you ask Beatrice?' She could also have said, 'I'll ask my mum.'

The two teenagers took the train, chatting about Amira along the way. Kleber wanted to know where she went to school, whether she was making any progress, whether she was happy. As the station drew closer, he fell silent.

'I hope I remember the way,' said Kleber when they were on the platform.

But he immediately recognised the big pond with its statues of rearing horses, the long avenue of over-hanging trees and the road that led up to Malicroix.

He rang the bell. When the door was opened, Zahra was amazed to see a huge carpeted hallway with discreet figures busying past. It was like a hotel. There was a woman under a sign that said *Reception*.

'I'm Mr Maluri,' Kleber introduced himself. 'I've come to pick my brother up for the weekend.'

'Have you?' she asked as if she very much doubted it.

She looked down at a register.

'You have,' she conceded, apparently with some regret. 'Room 112, on the first floor.'

Kleber opted to go up by the stairs, a white marble staircase, one of the vestiges of past splendour. One person went up, another came down, passing him in silence. Busy, busy. In the corridor Kleber saw a very old woman coming towards him, using the wall for support.

'Miss,' she called out to Zahra. 'My mother's in my room.'

'Your mother?' Zahra asked, amazed.

'It's not that I mind,' said the old lady. 'But she's dead.'

Kleber pulled Zahra by the arm and whispered, 'She's barking.'

A voice carried along the corridor, it was the supervisor for that floor: 'Mrs Lachaise! You've got out of your room again! I'll tell your mother, you know.'

Kleber quickened his pace and reached room 112. He knocked and, hearing no answer, went in.

'People!' cried a man of indeterminate age, who was already in his pyjamas.

'I'm so sorry, I've been given the wrong room number . . .'

'There's people, there's people, there's people,' the man said, punching his own head.

Kleber pushed Zahra out again.

'He's barking too.'

He stormed down to reception.

'My brother isn't in room 112.'

'Isn't he?' said the receptionist, increasingly doubtful that Kleber knew what he was talking about.

She looked down at her register again.

'Oh no. It's 212. Hurry up. We're about to close.'

Kleber decided to take a deep breath instead of yelling insults at her. On the second floor there was nothing but a nightlight on in the corridor. It was seven o'clock in the evening but it could have been the middle of the night. Malicroix residents had their last meal at six. They were in bed now.

Room 212. Kleber opened the door a crack. Sure enough, Simple was there, sitting on the bed with his jacket buttoned up all wrong and his bag of toys over his shoulder.

'Simple? I'm here. Hey! It's Kleber. Aren't you going to say hello?'

'There's snakes,' said Simple, not looking at his brother.

He pointed at the patterns on the bedside rug: Ever since the lady had dressed him, he'd been waiting there looking at the design on the carpet.

'Are you coming with us, Simple?' asked Zahra, shaking him by the shoulder. 'We're going to the flat.'

'They're snakes,' Simple whispered.

'Do you want to see Amira?'

Simple turned his eyes towards her, blue eyes that had lost all their sparkle.

'Can we go?' he said in a flat voice. 'I don't like anyone here.'

As they left the room, Kleber had a feeling he had forgotten someone. He stopped in the doorway.

'Have you got Mister Babbit?'

'No.'

'Where is he?'

Simple went straight over to the bedside table, opened the drawer and took out his cuddly toy. He handed it to his brother. Zahra let out a cry. The rabbit didn't have any eyes.

'What have you done?' cried Kleber.

'Mister Babbit doesn't want to see this, he doesn't.'

'Did you keep his eyes?' asked Zahra.

Simple nodded and patted his jacket pocket. Something clinked inside.

'Aria can sew them back on,' said Kleber. 'Let's go.'

On the stairs between the second and first floors they came across the old lady leaning against the wall.

'Miss,' she said to Zahra, 'my grandmother's in my bed. It's not that I mind but she's done a wee-wee.'

'Mrs Lachaise!' cried a voice from the floor above.

'That woman's such a pain,' said the old lady, and she carried on up the stairs as quickly as she could.

Simple recognised her as she passed. 'It's the old lady who scapes.'

As he closed the door to Malicroix, Kleber himself had a feeling of escaping. Simple gave no reaction to being outside, happy just to name everything he saw: 'Trees, horse statues, the cakery shop . . .'

At the station Kleber handed him a ticket.

'Shall I put it in the hole?'

'Yes, and go through the turnstile.'

'Whoosh! the ticket's gone. Peek-a-boo, there it is!'

The ticket disappearing in the slot, then reappearing brought the first smile to Simple's face.

When they went their separate ways, Zahra said to Kleber, 'You know, there's always someone at my house. If you want, we could have Simple for you on Wednesdays or Saturdays . . .'

She was suggesting he should give up on Malicroix. Kleber felt she was judging him and, instead of thanking her, he just groaned. Then, before he could stop himself, he kissed her on both cheeks. A soft perfume wafted round him, all vanilla and orange blossom.

'See you tomorrow?'

'Amira's going to be pleased,' Zahra replied.

Then, in her confusion, she bumped into the door as she turned away.

Enzo was in the apartment, zapping the TV, disgruntled as ever. Aria caught sight of him in the half-light of the living room as she headed to the kitchen for a glass of water. She slipped over to him, barefoot and wearing next to nothing as usual. Enzo pretended to be interested in a repeat of some lame detective series, but wasn't very convincing. Aria hopped on to the sofa and crouched next to him.

'Have you got a couple of minutes or is this too fascinating?'

Enzo put it on mute. His throat was gripped with panic. He could feel the warmth of her skin as clearly as if he were holding her.

'Simple's on his way home,' whispered Aria. 'I thought we could offer to help Kleber. If each of us did *something*, Simple could stay here. Don't you think?'

'Yup.'

He could barely unclamp his teeth.

'By the way, have you written any more of your book?'

'Yes.'

'Can I read it?'

He thought of everything he had put Emma through in the last fifty pages and sniggered.

'What does that mean?'

'It means "I give you a really hard time".'

220

'Well, that's nice.'

So near, so far. Between their bodies lay the king's sword.

'What are you thinking about?' whispered Aria.

'Tristan and Isolde.'

'Do you really love me . . . that much?' she asked with a throaty laugh.

'You know I do.'

'What about Stephanie?'

He shrugged but didn't deign to reply.

'Emmanuel's asked me to marry him. Can you believe it?'

'Brilliant.'

'I said I'd think about it.'

'What about me, Aria . . .'

'You?'

'Do you want to marry me?'

They heard Kleber's key in the lock. Aria tried to make the most of it and get away, but Enzo snatched her arm firmly. 'Can I have an answer?'

'No.'

'You bitch,' he said, losing his temper. 'You little tease!'

He got a punch for that, but he returned it. They

were grappling with each other as the light flooded on.

'It's not good to fight,' said Simple, and Aria jumped up to give him a kiss.

'I'm so happy to see you!'

Simple pushed her away and pointed at Enzo. 'It's him, you should be kissing him. You're not nice.'

'That's just what I was saying,' said Enzo, tucking his shirt back into his trousers.

Hearing voices, Corentin came out of his bedroom.

'Hey, how's Mister Babbit, then?' he asked, chuffed to see the idiot again.

'He's lost his eyes,' Simple replied, handing the rabbit to Aria.

Seeing the blinded toy, the distraught flatmates were reduced to silence. Corentin cleared his throat. 'You know, Kleber, maybe we can get our act together so that we can keep Simple here?'

'I do bugger all on Mondays and Tuesdays,' added Enzo.

'I'm usually here on Saturdays,' said Aria.

'I'm meant to be picking up girls in the Tuileries Gardens on Sundays,' Corentin chipped in. 'But, given my success rate, I could take Simple with me.'

'You never know, it might work better,' offered Enzo.

Kleber started laughing, with tears in his eyes. Emmanuel, who had finally left his computer, suggested they all drank to Simple's return. Aria went to get a needle and thread to sew Mister Babbit's eyes back on. When she had finished, she said, 'Hello-o!', and waggled his ears.

She handed the toy back to Simple and wanted to give him another kiss. He pushed her away, apparently angry.

'You mustn't kiss me,' he said. 'He's the one who loves you,' he said, pointing at Enzo.

'Perfect,' said Emmanuel, storming out of the living room. 'Even Simple can tell.'

When Kleber took Simple over to Zahra's house the next day, he found the whole family ready for action. Their mum had made pastries, their dad had dug out his old hookah to entertain Simple, the girls had gathered together all their toys, Djemilah had surreptitiously put on some make-up, Leila had applied three layers of strawberry lipgloss and Amira was dressed up as a blue fairy.

223

'It's all too beautiful,' said Simple. Everyone laughed.

'Mister Babbit! Mister Babbit!' cried the younger girls.

Simple gave a pout, looked at the ceiling and swayed from side to side; Kleber couldn't believe he was milking it so much. Eventually, he thrust his hand into his pocket, opened his eyes wide with horror and cried, 'He's gone.'

Everyone was very worried.

'Hello-o!' roared Simple, brandishing his rabbit by the ears.

Everyone clapped. Amira kissed Mister Babbit and carried him triumphantly on her head all the way to the dining room, where tea was ready.

'Will you stay?' Zahra asked Kleber shyly.

'No . . . I . . . no.'

He had a date with Beatrice. He was almost sorry not to be eating the delicious cakes. But he was hopeful that he might finally get what he so desperately wanted.

'I won't be long,' he said, blushing.

Which was something of a boast. He spent the end of the afternoon chatting and fondling, without making significant progress.

'Already?' asked Simple when his brother came to pick him up.

'Sorry,' Kleber grunted sarcastically.

'Will you stay for some *mezze*?' asked their mother, who had been cooking all day.

'Yes, yes!' begged the girls.

'You must make the most of the good things in life,' Mr Larbi told him. '"All good things come from God." It's in the Koran.'

Kleber accepted the invitation, unaware that Mr Larbi was planning to appraise him. During the course of the meal he turned and nodded to his wife several times. The boy seemed well brought up. He liked Lebanese food. He served his brother before himself. And Mr Larbi nodded some more. That was good, very good. Zahra was ashamed. How could she make her parents understand that she loved Kleber but Kleber didn't love her?

After dinner, Zahra saw the two boys to the front door. A little wave from Djemilah was enough to keep all the others in the living room.

'Simple can come whenever he likes,' said Zahra in a shaky voice. 'I hope he feels at home here.'

Kleber thanked her politely and kissed her on both

cheeks. Zahra had wanted to add, 'And I hope you feel at home here too,' but her lips had stayed closed.

'Zahra's nice,' said Simple on the stairs.

'Mm,' was all Kleber managed to say.

He knew that Zahra was in love with him. But he would see about that later.

'Beatrice isn't nice,' he added.

'It's not as simple as that.'

'But I'm Simple.'

'Well, my name's Complicated.'

On Sunday morning, Corentin took Simple for a jog. He came back quite out of breath.

'It's not funny,' he complained. 'Corentin kept running the whole time. I couldn't catch him.'

After lunch, Simple played in the living room while Enzo wrote. Like in the good old days. Aria and Emmanuel disappeared for the whole day. Towards the end of the afternoon, Corentin and Enzo asked Kleber if they could go to the cinema.

'Guys, you can do whatever you like!'

'You're . . . you're not taking Simple back to Malicroix, are you?' Corentin mumbled.

'Never.'

Just before supper time, Kleber noticed there wasn't any bread.

'I'm nipping to the baker. Do you want to come with me, Simple?'

'Mister Babbit's feet are hurting.'

'OK.'

The first bakery was closed. Fate hangs on so little. Kleber had to go further. On the way back he suddenly felt worried. He hurried, raced up the stairs.

'Simple, I've got the bread! Simple?'

On the dining room table was a scribbled post-it note. Kleber recognised his father's writing: *Came by for Simple after all. See you leave him on his own. He'll be better off at Malicroix at weekends.*

Chapter 12

Where Mister Babbit finds
a way out

Mr Maluri had wanted to spare Kleber a painful scene. But Simple didn't react at all when they arrived at Malicroix. He seemed indifferent, as if he had withdrawn deep inside himself. *That's an improvement*, thought Mr Maluri.

As soon as his father had left, Simple lay his rabbit on his pillow and went to fetch his craft scissors.

'Are you going to take my eyes out again?'

'You mustn't see this.'

'Yes, but how am I going to cry?' asked Mister Babbit.

Simple thought for a moment, toying with the scissors. It was a good question. He sat down on the bed, leant his head against the wall and let two tears spill down.

'Kleber's a bastard,' said Mister Babbit.

But all of them, all of them had betrayed him, Enzo, Aria, Corentin, Zahra. All of them had abandoned him. And Kleber. Specially Kleber.

'Mrs Lachaise!' cried a voice in the distance.

Simple leapt to his feet and opened his door. The old lady was right there, clinging to the wall.

'Come in here, old lady,' whispered Simple. 'Come and hide.'

The old lady went in without a moment's thought.

'Mrs Lachaise!' cried the supervisor.

'Oh, she really can be a pain,' the incorrigible escapee confided to Simple.

'She won't find you.'

Simple put a finger to his lips. They both listened as the supervisor's footsteps faded.

'Why've you got a name you can sit on?' Simple asked.

The old lady didn't seem at all surprised.

'It's from my husband's family. My husband was Lachaise.'

Simple gave a great smile of delight at the thought.

'And have you got children?'

229

'A grown-up son. But he's mean. He shut me up in here.'

'It's my brother what did me.'

'But I'm going to escape.'

'Me too. But I'm not going to scape to the stairs. I'm going to scape to the street, I am.'

'Really?'

'Do you want to scape with me?'

Mrs Lachaise seemed to gather up what was left of her common sense.

'I won't be able to walk far. You're good and young. How old are you?'

'Twelve.'

'That's young,' Mrs Lachaise said thoughtfully.

Meanwhile, the supervisor was growing concerned. Usually, 'the daft old bird', as she called her, didn't go further than the third floor. But even the corridor on the fourth floor was deserted. Where had she gone? The supervisor went back down to reception.

'Hey, keep an eye out,' she told her colleague. 'I can't find old ma Lachaise. Don't let her get out.'

* * *

230

In room 212, Simple's plan to run away was coming together.

'Have you got any money?' asked the old lady. 'Because you need a lot of that in life.'

Simple felt thwarted by this information. But Mrs Lachaise took from her pocket a few coins wrapped in a banknote acting as a purse.

'Paper money!' Simple gasped in wonder.

This present gave him an idea.

'I'm going to be Mr Mutchbinguen.'

He put on his suit and Mrs Lachaise tied his tie for him. He put Mister Babbit in one pocket and his vevolver in the other.

'So, aren't you coming?'

'Another time,' said the old lady. 'Can I stay in your room in the meantime? My grandfather's in mine and he smokes a pipe.'

'You can have my room, Mrs Lachaise.'

While this arrangement was being reached so easily, a degree of panic was spreading through the Malicroix staff. Everyone was looking for the escapee. Simple came out of his room, went down the stairs and ended up in the hall without anyone turning a hair.

'Would you mind leaving straight away, sir,' said the woman on reception, not really paying attention. 'We're just closing.'

Simple didn't wait to be asked again. He almost ran to the door. Once outside, he had a shock: it was dark.

'There's lamps,' he reassured himself, seeing the streetlights.

He started walking and found his way by listing the things he had noticed the previous time: 'Trees, horse statues, the cakery shop. I'm hungry, I am.'

His father hadn't thought to ask whether he had had supper.

A pool of light on the pavement attracted his attention. There was a private view in a picture gallery. As it was mild for the time of year, people were drifting in and out of the doorway, holding glasses. Simple pressed his face up to the window.

'Nibbles!'

Mr Mutchbinguen made straight for the buffet. One woman was working her way through all the snacks, and Simple gave her an encouraging smile. He took a little square of bread with some salmon on it, peeled it and put the salmon down on the edge of the tray. The woman watched the procedure, dumbstruck. Simple popped the bread in his mouth, then grabbed the salted peanuts, and went off to look at the paintings, regularly delving into the bowl.

Two enlightened enthusiasts were studying one of Mr N'Guyen Tuan's canvases.

'I prefer his green period. He commits absolute lunacy with lichen. This is good, but it's more . . .'

'It's more consensual.'

The two enlightened enthusiasts noticed Mr Mutchbinguen's intrusive presence as he viewed the painting with a critical expression. They waited for the pearls of wisdom this authority would pronounce.

'I do rabbits,' said Simple.

The two men gave embarrassed coughs and watched Simple walk away.

'Ah, thank you, orange juice!'

A waiter was passing with a tray.

'It's punch, sir.'

'I know this stuff,' said Simple, 'it makes your head spin.'

He drank what turned out to be only slightly alcoholic orange juice, then went to give his glass back to the waiter.

'Thank you. But you're a liar, this isn't punch.'

Gradually, all eyes turned on Simple. He went from one group of people to another, smiling amiably. He latched on to a gaggle of women chatting quietly.

'I really like his female nudes from the early days,' said one.

'I don't think his wife was so keen on them,' said another with a laugh. 'Apparently, he goes at it like a rabbit with whoever he can lay his hands on . . .'

Hearing this word, Simple smiled mischievously and put his hand in his pocket.

'Hello-o,' he said.

He gave a little pause for suspense, then brandished his rabbit by the ears. 'It's Mister Babbit!'

The women scattered. Then, as Mr N'Guyen Tuan's friends and acquaintances preferred consensus to lunacy, the two waiters took Simple by the arms and put him out on the street. Simple wandered off having not understood a thing, except that none of those people liked rabbits.

'Who cares!' Mister Babbit consoled himself. 'We're off to Paris.'

They were outside the station.

'You need a quicket.'

'Just jump the barrier,' said Mister Babbit. 'Hup! It's not high.'

Simple took Mister Babbit's advice and, without a ticket, stepped on to a random train, which took him to Châtelet station in the heart of Paris.

'Here we are,' he said off the top of his head.

When he found himself in the middle of the city in the middle of the night, Simple felt suffocatingly small.

'It's Mr Mutchbinguen . . . He's going to Paris.'

He went over to a group of young men who had had a bit too much to drink and were talking loudly, slurring their words.

'Excuse me, hello, how are you?' Simple said earnestly. 'Which way's Paris please?'

The lads gave a loud, stupid laugh.

'What sort of loser are you? Have you lost your mummy?'

'You haven't got ten euros to spare, have you?'

'Does euros mean money?' asked Simple.

The quips started flying.

'He's got an IQ of two!'

'Have you seen the face on him?'

'And the twat just stands there smiling!'

The smile fell from Simple's face. He wanted to carry on on his way, but one of the men caught him by the collar. 'You sure you haven't got ten euros? Have a good look in your pockets.'

Anger boiled over from Simple's heart to his head.

'I've got my knife, I have! I'm going to war!'

Another lad took out a flick knife.

'Leave him to me,' he said to the one holding Simple.

'I've got my vevolver!' cried Simple, taking it from his pocket.

'Fuck, he's got a gun!'

The lout loosened his grip and Simple broke free. He ran without looking where he was going, through a muddle of streets and side streets, moaning, 'Kleber,' every now and then.

When he slowed down, he was on the Place de la République. He looked around and murmured despondently, 'This isn't Paris.'

He carried on walking because he didn't know what else to do. His anger had subsided, leaving a great frozen desert inside him. He went back the way he had come, taking different streets. His stomach was tormented by hunger. He stood dreamily outside

236

food shops that were still open, and drooled at the smell from fast food outlets. He eventually stopped outside a restaurant where a hippopotamus beckoned him in. Inside, a hostess in a black skirt and white blouse was waiting to seat customers.

'Are you on your own, sir?'

Jenny was doing her first work experience in hotel and catering. She was a bit apprehensive.

'No, I'm with Mister Babbit.'

'I see. Two of you, then ... Would you like to follow me?' she recited as she had been taught to on her hospitality course.

'Where are we going?'

'Smoking or non-smoking?'

This question worried Simple.

'It's not me, it's Mister Babbit.'

'He doesn't smoke?' Jenny assumed.

'No, he pukes.'

She raised an eyebrow; his answer wasn't in her repertoire. She seated her peculiar customer in the non-smoking area.

'Would you rather wait for your friend before ordering?'

'Kleber does ordering.'

'Oh. Will there be three of you?'

'Twelve.'

Jenny felt that her training had not prepared her for every eventuality.

'Excuse me. I'll be right back.'

Simple took Mister Babbit from his pocket, tied a serviette round his neck and sat him down at a plate. Then he got up to take a piece of bread from a neighbouring table. The man almost leapt out of his skin. 'Help yourself, why don't you?!'

'You've still got loads!' retorted Simple, pointing at the basket.

He was nibbling the crust when the head waiter came over.

'Mister Babbit's hungry, he is,' he told him, nodding at his cuddly toy.

'Yes . . . Excuse me. I'm going to ask you to kindly move along.'

'To smoking?'

'Outside.'

'But I haven't eaten, I haven't.'

'Outside!' the head waiter insisted.

His tone had become threatening. Customers at nearby tables were watching now.

'Not all loonies are shut away,' said the man at the next table.

Simple took Mister Babbit and ran for the exit. It may have been the middle of the night but the truth was dawning on him: it wasn't rabbits that people didn't like – it was him.

In the apartment that Monday morning, Simple wasn't what everyone was thinking about. Emmanuel announced to Enzo and Corentin that he was leaving.

'You two are going?' asked Corentin, very surprised that his sister hadn't mentioned anything.

'*I'm* going,' corrected Emmanuel. 'For now, I'm going back to my parents. I should think you couldn't give a stuff.'

He looked pointedly at Enzo.

'I'm going to look for a studio. Aria's meant to be joining me there.'

Enzo didn't show a flicker of reaction. But as soon as he could he ran to see Mr Villededieu.

'George!'

'Has she said yes?'

'No. Not yet.'

Enzo had become his elderly neighbour's favourite

239

soap opera. When he heard that Emmanuel was leaving, he gave a victorious cheer.

'Hey, hang on, it might not mean anything. He's putting pressure on Aria.'

'You do the same.'

'How?'

George thought. All the good old techniques – the photo of a rival left lying around, suicide threats – seemed beneath his young friend.

'Enzo, have you finished your novel?'

'Not quite.'

'Finish it and give it to your Aria. But watch out, it has to have a happy ending. Lorenzo proposes to Emma and she says yes.'

Enzo pulled a face.

'That's a bit cheesy.'

'Listen, my boy, I don't read *Marie-Claire* but I can tell you a thing or two. Love *is* a bit cheesy.'

Enzo went back up to the apartment feeling very happy. The end of his novel was in sight. He wrote for a good hour, alone in the apartment. Then the telephone rang.

'Hello, it's Mrs Bardoux from social services. Could I speak to Kleber please?'

'He's at college. What do you want from him now?'

'He needs to be informed. His brother has disappeared.'

The news struck Kleber like a thunderbolt. The staff at Malicroix noticed that Simple was missing when the time came for his morning wash. Sleeping in his bed where he should have been was an old lady they had been looking for all night. As for Simple, he had escaped.

'He can't have gone far without any money,' said Enzo. 'And he doesn't know how to get around.'

Kleber listened, his eyes wide with terror.

'This is terrible,' he murmured. 'He's . . . he's like a child. He's three years old, Enzo.'

'Calm down. We'll find him. They've told your dad. They'll look for him. He doesn't exactly go unnoticed, does he?'

Mrs Bardoux had promised to ring back as soon as there was any news. But the afternoon trickled by with nothing but a phone call from Mr Maluri threatening to sue Malicroix if anything happened to his son.

Aria, Corentin and Enzo kept Kleber company. The waiting was becoming unbearable.

'Go out and get some air,' Corentin encouraged him. 'If we hear anything, we'll call you on your mobile.'

Kleber ran to the end of lessons at college so he could let Zahra know.

'Oh, there you are!' said Beatrice. 'We saw you scarpering like a rabbit at lunchtime.'

The word 'rabbit' brought tears to Kleber's eyes.

'Is everything OK?'

'It's my brother . . .'

'Again! When's he going to leave you in peace –'

Kleber spotted Zahra. He unceremoniously dumped Beatrice.

'Zahra!'

They left together and Kleber poured out his heart to her. He felt guilty. He shouldn't have let Simple go back to Malicroix. If anything happened to his brother, he would never forgive himself.

'Do you have faith?'

'Sometimes.'

'Ask Him to bring your brother back.'

'I don't think God intervenes in people's lives. That's a childish concept.'

'Ask God to bring your brother back.'

'Oh God, please bring Simple back,' said Kleber.

He laughed with tears in his eyes. 'Sounds like I'm asking Him to make everything simple again . . . maybe I am.'

Meanwhile, Enzo and Corentin clucked round the telephone like mother hens.

'Isn't life weird?' Corentin philosophised. 'A couple of weeks ago, Simple got on my nerves. Now, he's like a brother. Fuck, if they don't find him . . .'

'You're a bundle of laughs, aren't you,' Enzo grunted.

All at once the front door slammed. They thought it was Kleber. But Emmanuel shot past the living room.

'He's come to pick up his stuff,' Corentin commentated.

Half an hour later, Emmanuel still hadn't come back out of the bedroom; Aria was in there too. *He's 'putting pressure on her'*, thought Enzo. When Kleber arrived home, he could only offer him half-hearted support. Enzo was on the alert, hoping to hear raised voices, a good row. 'Bugger off, bugger off,' he kept saying inside his head, wanting to drive Emmanuel away with his thoughts.

Kleber went and collapsed on his bed saying, 'Come back, come back,' over and over in his head.

It was getting dark outside and in their hearts. Kleber had never felt so distraught. Emmanuel left the apartment. Alone.

Enzo jumped up from the sofa and snuck over to Aria's door. He listened, and thought he heard crying. He couldn't be sure. He knocked. She was on the bed with her head in her pillow. She turned to Enzo. Yes, she was crying.

'Oh, for God's sake, piss off! I don't need you!'

'I'm sorry,' Enzo stammered. 'I didn't want to . . .'

He closed the door, gutted. He wanted to go and get help from his elderly neighbour. But he didn't dare because of Simple. Find Simple first.

Simple had been all over Paris from north to south and east to west. He had walked all day with no food or drink. He had slept a bit on a bench. He was trying to find Paris, where Kleber lived. Sometimes he cried. He wanted to die, but he didn't know how to go about it. Mister Babbit had retreated to the depths of his pocket.

'It's night time,' Simple said, though it had been dark for a long time.

He was in his own neighbourhood but didn't recognise it. He stopped outside the Vieux Cardinal Hotel. *Rooms to let by the week*, said a little sign. Simple couldn't read but the splodges of rust on the sign were associated with his brother in his memory.

'Are you looking for love, bunny rabbit?' said a voice cloaked in cigarette smoke.

In other circumstances, Simple would have brandished Mister Babbit. Now he settled for twiddling the rabbit's ears inside his pocket. The girl who was leaning up against the door tried to hook her customer.

'What's your name?'

'I'm Mr Mutchbinguen.'

The girl threw her head back to laugh freely.

'Haven't you got a nickname?'

Simple thought. 'It's Mutch.'

Another girl came out of the seedy hotel and looked Simple over.

'Oh, I see you've got company . . . Hello, sweetheart.'

'I'm Mutch,' said Simple.

Much *what*, exactly? The girls caught one another's eye. The boy looked a bit washed up. Did he have any money? The second girl put her arms around his neck.

'What do you want?'

'My brother.'

She quickly unhooked the necklace made by her arms and turned to her friend.

'Hey, he's an idiot.'

'I've got learning difficulties,' corrected Simple.

'We're not going to get much out of this,' said the first girl, with a disgusted pout.

'That depends,' said the other girl. She turned back to Simple. 'You got any money?'

Simple had learned to be wary. He shook his head.

'Kleber's got money. He's in Paris.'

His lips were quivering.

'Do you know where Paris is?'

'He's lost,' said the girl. 'You're lost, aren't you?'

Simple nodded. Something started stirring in the two girls' hearts. They put their arms round Simple.

'Have you got any papers?'

Simple looked surprised, rummaged in a pocket and produced an old bubblegum wrapper. They laughed, more touched than they would have thought possible.

'Hold on, I'll give you a hand,' said the one who had first hooked him, a blonde who was a bit jaded beneath her make-up.

She searched through the other pocket, which had a hole in it and was where Mister Babbit was buried like a rabbit in a burrow.

'What's this, then?' asked the blonde, pulling on the ears.

'It's Mister Babbit,' mumbled Simple.

The girl shook her head as if to say, 'What a sad case!', and handed the cuddly toy to her friend.

'Hang on to that. I'll have a look through the jacket. Hey, don't cry . . .'

Tears were rolling down Simple's cheeks. The girl carried on with her inventory of his pockets.

'Look at this! A revolver!'

'It's fake,' said Simple. 'I haven't got a knife, I haven't.'

'He's even got some dosh. Seventeen euros.'

'The boy's loaded!' sniggered the other girl, lighting a cigarette.

Eventually, the blonde delved into the inside pocket of Simple's jacket. Simple had an identity card in a plastic wallet.

'Barnaby Maluri, that's his name.'

She handed the card to her friend along with the money and the revolver. Just to be thorough, she went through the last pocket, and took out a piece of card on which Kleber had written. *I answer to the name Simple. I have learning difficulties. In case of emergency, call my brother on mobile . . .*

Without a word, the girl handed the card to her friend. A strange feeling washed over her, reminding her of childhood heartache. With the back of her hand, she wiped Simple's cheeks.

'Hey, I said don't cry. We're going to call your brother. OK?'

Simple nodded, then pointed shyly at Mister Babbit. 'Can I have him back?'

The two girls put everything back where it belonged in his pockets and nestled the rabbit in his hands.

'I'll call him,' said the blonde, taking out her mobile.

Kleber had fallen asleep in an armchair. His mobile's ringtone startled him.

'Hello? Yes, I'm Kleber.'

'We've got your brother,' said a strangely muffled sounding woman's voice.

248

'Simple? Where?'

'At the Vieux Cardinal Hotel. I'll tell you where it is . . .'

'You don't need to! I know. I'll be there in two minutes. Oh my God!'

He ran to the door, threw himself into the stairwell, and hurtled down the street.

'Oh, holy fuck,' he said between his teeth.

There he was, between two girls, with his rabbit in his hands.

'Simple! Simple!'

Kleber hugged him and just kept saying, 'Oh my God! Oh, fuck . . .'

He eventually managed to calm down. He looked at the two prostitutes.

'I don't know how to thank you.'

'D'you need anything else?' joked the blonde.

'No, thanks, I'm fine . . .'

The two brothers walked up the Rue du Cardinal-Lemoine hand in hand.

'I'm hungry,' Simple said in a small voice.

His legs could barely carry him.

Chapter 13

Where Mister Babbit dies

'It's the shock.'

The doctor could find no other explanation for the hallucinations that gripped Simple for three whole days. The flatmates took it in turns to watch over him. One morning, when it was Corentin's turn, he glanced over at Simple, who seemed to be sleeping, then sat down in the armchair.

'Where's Mister Babbit?' came a voice.

Corentin leapt up from his seat, as if it had just stung him. Simple was sitting up, his hair wilder than usual, its straw colour set alight by the blue of his eyes.

'How are you, mate? You recognise me, don't you? It's Corentin.'

'Where's Mister Babbit?'

Corentin got the decrepit-looking toy from the shelf. Simple took it and put it down in from of him, a peculiar sadness in his eyes.

'Why're people nasty to Mister Babbit?'

Simple was always saying things that really got to Corentin, who turned away to wipe his eyes.

'It's not . . . it's not really that they're nasty. But people don't understand Mister Babbit. He's . . . he's too different from them. With his big ears and . . . um . . . his whiskers. You see, he's a rabbit . . .'

'A talking rabbit,' Simple helped him.

'Well, that's right. People find it amazing, a bit frightening.'

Simple sighed. 'It's clompicated.'

'Well, you just stay Simple. Who gives a toss what other people think!'

'Uh-oh, bad word.'

Corentin ran to tell Enzo in the living room. 'He's cured!'

'These things happen.'

This was all Mrs Bardoux could find to say about Simple's escape.

'You know, in some places, they tie the residents

to their beds. That's no better. I do still think that Malicroix is, shall we say, a lesser evil.'

'I want what's best for my brother,' replied Kleber.

He was back in the little office lined with metal cupboards.

'We all want what's best for Simple, but it mustn't be at your expense.'

Kleber raised his voice. 'I'm happy living with Simple.'

'But think of the constant responsibility weighing down on you. You're a minor . . .'

'In ten days' time,' said Kleber, starting to laugh, 'you'll have an adult sitting opposite you.'

Mrs Bardoux nodded, but wasn't prepared to back down too quickly.

'You're young and idealistic. Don't think that I'm opposing you for the sake of it. I know, because I have a fair bit of experience of these situations, this kind of devotion comes at a very high price. Simple is completely dependent. Remember that some day you might want to get married, to have children . . .'

Kleber smiled, thinking of Zahra and her sisters. 'My children will love Simple because Simple's a child too,' he said, his face lighting up. He seemed to be defying every ounce of mediocrity in the world, and Mrs Bardoux looked away.

'I've done what I could to help you, Kleber. I thought I was doing the right thing . . .' she said.

'I know. Thank you.'

At the apartment, Aria told her brother that she was going to spend a few days in Paimpol with their parents.

'What about your course?'

'I can't seem to work any more.'

She looked really tired.

'Is it all over with Emmanuel?' Corentin dared to ask.

'I think so . . . He wanted me to say yes straight away. To go with him. But I didn't know . . . not any more . . .'

She seemed very sad.

'Will you come back for Kleber's birthday?'

'I'll try, Coco, I can't promise anything.'

That evening, Enzo finished his novel. When Aria wasn't in her bedroom, he nipped in there. He saw the suitcase open and half filled, and dropped his exercise book into it. On the first page he had written: *If you don't love me, destroy this.*

'Are you going away for ever and ever?' asked Simple.

Aria was fastening her suitcase.

'No, Simple. I'm going to get some rest at my mum and dad's.'

'My mummy, she's dead, she is, and my daddy, he doesn't love me.'

Aria put her arms round Simple's neck.

'*I'm* not your boyfriend,' he reminded her.

'I know. But you're my prince.'

And she kissed him.

The Larbi household was delighted to hear that Simple was home.

'Amira's so happy when she sees him,' Yasmine said.

Her husband nodded. Simple was a good boy. But the one he was thinking about was Kleber. He had grasped that Zahra liked him more than he liked her. Kleber just needed to mature a bit and, until he did, he mustn't be allowed to stray too far.

'We should do something to celebrate Zahra's birthday,' he said out of the blue.

'Again? It was last week.'

'Yes, but we only celebrated as a family. Nowadays, the young like inviting their friends over.'

'Zahra hasn't got that many. Apart from Simple and Kleber.'

Mr Larbi looked at his wife as if she had just made a very sensible suggestion.

'You're right. She can just invite Kleber and Simple. Next Saturday.'

Yasmine saw straight through this.

'There's a problem with Kleber.'

'What problem?' her husband asked anxiously.

'He goes to Mass.'

'Oh, that . . .' He smiled. '"The closest in friendship to Muslims are those who said: 'We are Christians.'" It's in the Koran.'

At first Kleber was delighted by Zahra's invitation, then a bit embarrassed. Because, in the meantime, Beatrice had invited herself to his apartment on the same Saturday. Kleber decided he would share himself out. From two till four, he would be with Zahra; from four till six, with Beatrice. His finer feelings for Zahra; everything else for Beatrice.

* * *

On the appointed day, Simple put on Mr Mutchbinguen's outfit, including, a bow tie. It looked like a wayward butterfly around his neck. Enzo, Corentin and Kleber were sitting in the living room admiring his appearance: the wild hair, shining eyes, lopsided jacket and pockets bulging with bits and bobs.

'I'm ready.'

Zahra's family were all very excited when Simple and Kleber arrived at the house.

'I love girls sooo much,' said Simple, forgetting his former reservations about the opposite sex.

Kleber took Zahra aside. 'I have to leave at four. I've got a meeting with social services. Nothing serious, some papers to sign about Simple . . .'

He was lying so badly that Zahra almost asked him whether social services had hairy armpits. But her feminine instincts told her to go about things another way.

'That's a shame,' she said. 'But what really matters is that Simple can stay all afternoon.'

Kleber felt piqued. With a glum expression, he went over to the giggling circle of girls round his brother.

'I'm talking a different language,' Simple boasted to him.

The younger girls were teaching sign language to Simple and Mister Babbit. Kleber carried on sulking for a while, but then he asked how to say 'I love you' in sign language. Zahra showed him how, putting her hand flat against her stomach and lifting it up towards her heart.

'The further you take your hand from your body, the stronger your love,' she said, making a big sweeping gesture herself.

Kleber sat cross-legged with Zahra and her sisters and let his hands talk. He jumped when, looking at his watch, he saw it was already twenty to four. He rushed off, then realised, once he was out on the street, that he was going to be early. He slowed down and as he passed his parish church he wondered if it was open. One of the side doors let him in. The cool shadows fell over his heart.

He dipped his hand into the font and made the sign of the cross. He had been making this gesture since he was a child, when his mother was alive. She died when Kleber was fourteen.

'Look after your brother,' she had said, 'and I'll be up there looking out for you.'

He went straight over to the statue of Saint Thérèse of Lisieux. He put two euros in the box, listened to them clink against other coins, then took a candle, a big one, and put the wick up to a flame.

Let Simple light it! a voice echoed inside him, and he remembered how he, the younger of the two, had let his older brother have the privilege of lighting the candle. Because the little one was the big one and the big one was the little one.

'Mum,' he said, looking at the statue.

As he walked away down the side aisle, he saw the confessional that Mister Babbit had used as a cave. He slipped in behind the curtain, and knelt down, a shiver running over his skin.

When he left the church, it was long past four o'clock. If Beatrice had seen Corentin at the flat, she was bound to have discovered that Kleber had been invited to Zahra's house. If Enzo had answered the door, he would have covered for him. But, one way or another, the time had been and gone. *I really am complicated*, Kleber thought as he walked back to Zahra's house.

'Already?' Simple was amazed.

But he didn't say anything else and, this time, Kleber stayed to eat the delicious cakes.

When he got to back to the apartment, Enzo called to him from the living room. 'Your girlfriend, the redhead, came by! Did you two have a date?'

Kleber nodded.

'I said you had an urgent meeting with social services about your brother and you were sorry.'

'Thanks.'

Kleber's birthday fell on the All Saints Day bank holiday, which was a Friday that year. The first part of the holiday was spent preparing for the party. Kleber wanted to make a dignified entry into adulthood. He invited Beatrice and Zahra, and Zahra asked if she could bring along Djemilah.

'Are you inviting Stephanie?' Corentin asked Enzo.

Enzo shot him a filthy look. Corentin was going to ask his cousin Alexei and the English girlfriend, as usual.

'We have to invite Hubert and Jean-Paul, obviously.'

The list gradually filled out, but there weren't many girls on it.

'What about Aria?' Enzo asked in a small voice.

Corentin screwed up his face doubtfully.

'Have you asked her?' Enzo said irritably.

'Yes, but . . .'

'But what?'

'She doesn't know. In the morning it's yes. By the evening it's no. I promise I'm really trying. Apparently she's not well.'

'What sort of not well?'

Corentin pulled a face again, seriously risking a punch from his friend.

'Give her a bit of time,' Mr Villededieu soothed him. 'She's only just split up. She can't throw herself into your arms overnight. It wouldn't be tactful, or lady-like.'

Enzo rubbed his shoulder without thinking.

'Aria isn't feminine, she's fatal.'

This time around, Simple was involved in the preparations. So much so he started talking about Kleber's birthday as if it were his own.

'What presents am I getting?' he asked his brother.

'What would you like?'

'A tephelone, a tevelision and a contuper.'

'That's all a bit expensive. How about a watch, would that do?'

'Yeeeees!'

'Shall I get you the hammer to go with it?

Simple understood the joke and burst out laughing.

'There isn't a lil'man,' he said.

He had grown up a lot.

'Have you noticed there's less and less talk about Mister Babbit,' Corentin pointed out.

'Simple doesn't need him so much,' said Kleber. 'He's got friends now.'

All the same, Mister Babbit got his whiskers in the chocolate mousse, helped himself to the carrot sticks, played with the food processor, and was constantly being told to behave himself.

'Stop it, Simple!'

'It's not me, it's –'

And all the others joined in: 'Mister Babbit!'

The night of the party finally arrived.

'You don't *have* to dress up as Prince Charming, you know?' said Kleber.

'It's Mr Mutchbinguen, he's forty-twelve years old. It's his plimshon.'

'And you don't *have* to talk a different language!'

The first to arrive at the party were, as usual, Jean-Paul and Hubert. They talked loudly and said far too many stupid things; in other words they were the basic ingredient without which no party could get off the ground. Then came Alexei, very depressed. He had just split up with his girlfriend. Enzo glowered furiously at this emotional clone of himself, then greeted the medical student from Emmanuel and Aria's course.

'I just can't believe it,' she said at least a dozen times about the couple's break-up. 'I just can't believe it.'

She told him that Aria was planning to move out to live with her and two other girls in a loft apartment in the Eleventh Arrondissement. Enzo resisted the urge to go downstairs in despair and tell Mr Ville-dedieu this latest disastrous news.

The living room and dining room gradually started to buzz. Kleber looked at his watch every five minutes.

'I haven't got a watch,' his brother reminded him discreetly.

Beatrice eventually arrived. She had swapped her top that hardly covered her top for bottoms that barely covered her bottom, only just held in place by a belt.

'Hey,' she said to Kleber, 'thanks a bunch for leaving me in the lurch on Saturday.'

He was a little stunned by her aggressive tone.

'Oh, come on, don't give me that frightened rabbit face!' she cried.

'Hello-o!' said Mister Babbit, waggling his ears under her nose.

Beatrice brushed him away so harshly that Simple ran for cover.

'I had some urgent stuff to sort out, sorry,' Kleber replied curtly. 'Ah, there's Zahra!'

Zahra had just arrived, with Djemilah hot on her heels. She eyed her rival and stifled a sigh. Having nothing more sophisticated in her wardrobe, she was wearing her off-the-shoulder little black dress again.

'You look gorgeous,' Kleber complimented her quietly. 'So, your sister's decided against the chador, then?'

Djemilah had even put on Leila's skirt, which was a very mini mini on her.

'She's thought it over. Religion is in your heart, not on your head.'

Kleber nodded agreement and started unwrapping the presents that were piling up by the buffet. Beatrice had given him a pair of boxer shorts with a little pocket for condoms.

'Thanks,' said Kleber, hastily rolling them back up in the paper.

Zahra had found a pretty picture frame.

'It needs a picture of you in it,' suggested Kleber.

That was when Beatrice realised she had lost the fight.

'What about me, where's my presents?' Simple fretted.

Zahra then handed him a parcel festooned in bows. Simple tore it open.

'Clothes for little dwarves!'

It was a tiny jacket and a tiny pair of trousers in black felt with red trimmings and gold buttons, all made by her mother to cover up Mister Babbit's worn fur. Zahra helped Simple get his toy dressed, then everyone came to admire him.

'Mister Babbit looks wicked!' said Simple.

'It was bound to happen,' Enzo lamented. 'He's spent so much time with students, he talks like them now.'

Meanwhile, Djemilah had decided not to lose any time. After a good look round and using a process of elimination, she had identified Corentin as the prime candidate. She fired a first volley of questions at him: 'What are you studying? How old are you? Is she your girlfriend? What sort of music do you like?'

When the answers proved satisfactory, she introduced herself. She was in her last year at school and hoping to go on to do a diploma in public hygiene. Then she drank from the same glass as Corentin to read his thoughts, and managed to invite herself to have the first slow dance with him. Zahra watched her out of the corner of her eye, secretly horrified.

'I see your sister's emancipated herself pretty quickly,' Kleber commented.

'She's fourteen . . .'

Kleber decided to warn Enzo off, it was the best he could do.

'Enzo, you need to tell Corentin . . .'

'I'm not sure there's much we can tell Corentin right now.'

'The girl he's dancing with . . .'

'You mean the one who's stuck to him like a limpet?'

'Yes. She's fourteen.'

'Really?' said Enzo, genuinely surprised.

But he pulled himself together. 'Don't worry about it, Kleber. Corentin's not a fast mover. By the time he's got his act together, she'll be practically a pensioner.'

You couldn't get much out of Enzo on an evening like this. He made up his own mind that he was an outcast from society, and went and slumped on the sofa next to Alexei, who was already pretty inebriated.

'Life, you know what I'm saying, life's a bitch,' Alexei told him, his voice claggy. 'And there's . . . there's only one way to get over it, to get over this bitch, only one way!'

He raised his voice as if Enzo were trying to contradict him.

'No, there's no two ways. Only one. One way!'

Just then, someone rang the doorbell and Enzo would never find out how you got over life. Because Aria stepped into the living room.

Enzo didn't recognise her straight away. She had completely changed. Hair done, make-up on, elegant clothes. A woman. As if she wanted Enzo to gauge the vast distance between them. Hesitantly, he went over to her and stood there looking at her without a word.

'Good evening would be nice . . .' she said with her usual abruptness.

'If you can call it a good evening,' replied Enzo, mimicking Eeyore's gloomy voice.

'You're so silly . . .'

She went to kiss all her friends hello. And Simple. Specially Simple.

'So, you're part of the party then?'

'It's my plimshon.'

'That means "birthday",' translated Kleber.

Enzo had thought that he would be over the moon to see Aria back. But he just stood in the middle of the living room, moping and slightly drunk. He went off to lie down on his bed. He was about to fall asleep, fed up with everything but mostly himself, when someone knocked on the door. He lifted himself on to his elbows and a headache started banging against his temples like the clapper in a bell.

'What the hell?' he yelled.

Aria came in, closed the door and leant up against it.

'What?' Enzo repeated more gently.

She threw something next to his pillow.

'What's that?'

'What you wanted. Your book.'

Enzo didn't seem to understand.

'I've typed out your book, Enzo. It's on that memory stick.'

'Why did you do that?'

She sat down on the edge of the bed.

'Because I'm in love with your book. With your characters. With your central character.'

She would have liked to make the vertigo of this moment last a bit longer, standing at the top of the cliff. But the wave rising up from the depths of her stomach pushed her down on to the bed next to Enzo.

'Aria, Aria, really? Me? You're so beautiful this evening. I would never . . .'

'I'm beautiful for you.'

He hugged her, closing his eyes. Oh, Enzo, Enzo, how wonderful to have been so miserable!

'I love you, you have no idea how much I love you!'

She laughed and started tickling him. That made

him laugh too. Then they undressed each other, haphazardly, still tickling each other as they went.

'Are you making love?'

Enzo had just unzipped his fly. He sat up, breathlessly. Mister Babbit had popped his head round the door.

'Simple!'

'Yes?'

Simple put his head round the door too, as if he had been invited.

'Aren't you ashamed of yourself?' scolded Aria.

'No.'

He waggled his rabbit's ears.

'Mister Babbit likes watching, he does.'

Then they heard Corentin from the corridor. 'Come, Enzo, get your arse back here, it's time for the cake!'

Eventually everybody gathered back in the living room. They switched off the lights and Zahra carried in the cake with its eighteen candles, singing, 'Happy plimshon to you . . .'

'Happy plimshon, dear Kleber . . .' everyone joined in enthusiastically.

Everyone? No. Beatrice wasn't singing; her lips were clamped together with rage. She decided to sneak out of the room while the lights were out. But just as she was leaving, she spotted Mister Babbit, sitting forgotten on a beanbag. She felt she had a score to settle with the rabbit. She bent down, picked it up and headed off towards the kitchen. With two swift moves, the deed was done.

While this was going on, Corentin was slicing the cake.

Kleber gestured Simple over to join him in a quiet corner of the living room. He took off the watch on his own wrist and put it on his brother's.

'Is it mine for me?'

'You won't break it?'

Simple shook his head and watched the second hand scuttling round, apparently mesmerised.

'So, what's the time, Simple?' asked Enzo.

'Twelve.'

The local church clock struck midnight.

The party went on a bit longer. Simple fell asleep on the floor, Alexei sat on the sofa nursing his glass of wine, and Kleber and Corentin took Zahra and Djemilah home. Enzo and Aria snuck off to bed again.

*   *   *

270

'Mister Babbit's gone!'

Hearing his brother, Kleber lurched awake.

'What is in now? Can't you sodding leave me in peace with your Babbit?'

'He's gone.'

'No he hasn't, he's somewhere in all this muddle from the party.'

An hour later, Kleber embarked on a search. He soon had help from Corentin.

'Where did you leave him, can you remember?'

'There,' said Simple, pointing to the beanbag.

Enzo and Aria were alerted to the situation. The whole apartment was searched. Alexei, who had finished his nursing, sat up on the sofa.

'What are you looking for?'

'The cuddly rabbit.'

'Have to ask that girl, the redhead . . .'

'Beatrice?'

Alexei nodded.

'She took the rabbit from that beanbag. I thought it was weird, but I wasn't in a fit state to do much about it . . .'

Kleber felt spiteful anger wash over him. He narrowed his eyes intently.

'I'm going over to her place.'

Enzo held him back by the arm.

'Hey, hang on, you could call her. You're angry, Kleber. Let me do it.'

Enzo went off by himself to make the call, then came back.

'It was definitely her,' he said melodramatically. 'She chucked him down the waste disposal.'

The flatmates looked at each other, devastated.

'Well, we'll have to go and look for him,' said Simple.

'Of course, we're being stupid!' said Kleber, getting a grip.

They belted down the stairs and stormed into the dustbin area, just as the concierge was bringing the bins back inside.

'Oh holy cow! The bin men got here first,' said Enzo, more melodramatic by the minute.

'Did Mister Babbit get out of the dustbin?'

How would they get Simple to accept that his rabbit could never be found?

Back in the living room, he sat down on the beanbag.

'I'm going to wait for him here.'

'There's no point. He's in the bin lorry,' Enzo said.

'He'll scape.'

'No, that's not possible, he's a toy. He's not a real rabbit.'

'Yes he is,' Simple insisted stubbornly, his eyes brimming with tears, but he refused to let himself cry, rigid with determination.

In the end Aria hugged him to her and whispered in his ear, 'Simple, I know you love Mister Babbit. We all love Mister Babbit. But you'll just have to accept that Mister Babbit is dead.'

Simple started shaking.

'Like Mummy?'

'Like Mummy.'

He clasped his hands together.

'I want to be dead with them.'

'What about me, what about me?' cried Kleber, kneeling down before his brother. 'Do you want me to be all on my own?'

'You can just call Zahra on the tephelone.'

Kleber took his advice and called Zahra on the tephelone. She was there almost immediately.

'We'll get another one,' she told Simple. 'Another Mister Babbit.'

Simple flashed a reproachful look at her.

'He's the only one.'

And that was something everyone already knew.

On the floor below, Mr Villededieu was unaware of the drama affecting his neighbours but he was cursing them.

'That's it. They've gone and blocked the rubbish chute again. They say it's not them. But I can't think who else it could be!'

George had perfected a technique for unblocking the rubbish chute. He attached a 5 kg weight to the end of a piece of string and dropped it down the chute. That was enough to get whatever was blocking the way to tumble on down.

'There we are,' he said, hearing the tumbling sound of the rubbish.

What does fate hang on? Mr Villededieu wanted to prove the point that it really was the flatshare who were to blame so he went down to where the bins were.

A few minutes later he was ringing the bell to their apartment.

'This time,' he told Enzo, 'you'll have to admit that

it's you lot who block the rubbish chute with your crap!'

Enzo's eyes opened wide.

'George!' he cried and, with a melodramatic flourish, he added, 'You've saved our lives . . .'

'Is that idiot here, then?' bellowed the old man, coming into the living room.

Simple was huddled on the beanbag, with all his friends around him. George came forward solemnly and the others stepped aside so that Simple could see.

'Mister God!'

In the crook of George's arm, nestled like an ailing child, was a resuscitated Mister Babbit.

'Your rabbit reeks, you know,' he said, handing it back to Simple.

They all busied around. The tiny jacket and trousers were washed, Mister Babbit was shampooed and perfumed. Aria gave him a few stitches. Simple didn't do anything, but kept consulting his watch and looking important.

At the end of the afternoon, Zahra had to go home.

'Could we walk along by the river?' suggested Kleber. 'And talk a bit.'

He remembered saying the same sort of thing to Beatrice. *But that was different*, he thought, listening to his own footsteps echoing Zahra's. She was walking along beside him as she still would be in several years' time. Then children would walk with them, children who would love Simple because they would be simple in the way only children are.

Kleber was dreaming. He didn't agonise over whether or not he should put his arm around Zahra's waist or how to go about asking her for this or that. But their silence eventually made him feel awkward. He had promised to talk. He wanted to tell Zahra, 'I made a mistake, I thought I loved Beatrice, it's you that I love.' But surely there were different words to say it?

'Zahra, I wanted to tell you . . .'

She stopped and looked him right in the eye. She had been waiting for this moment. A mischievous smile suddenly transformed Kleber into Mister Babbit's younger brother.

'Listen to me, Zahra!'

He put his hand on his stomach, raised it up towards his heart then, with the tips of his fingers, touched Zahra's heart. Next, Zahra put her hand on her stomach, raised it up to her heart and the two of them put their arms around each other.

Back at the apartment, Enzo was lying on the sofa daydreaming, resting his head in Aria's lap.

'It's funny,' he said. 'I thought Simple wouldn't take his eyes off his rabbit all day. But the only thing he was interested in was his watch.'

'I think that, symbolically, Mister Babbit did die today,' said Aria, who was getting more and more interested in psychoanalysis. 'Simple won't ever claim he's alive again.'

'Don't you think that's sad?'

'Children grow up, Enzo. Is that sad?'

'Yes, it is. It's inevitable but it's sad.'

He looked up at Aria with his permanently worried expression, and she smiled at him. This was definitely the boy she loved.

Simple was in the bathroom. Facing him, hanging from the washing line by his ears, was a tattered, battered, stitched and stained cuddly toy.

'You dry yet?'

'My feet are still wet,' replied Mister Babbit.

'Did Beatrice throw you down the shooting place?'

'No, I did. I wanted to see the bin.'

Simple made an exaggerated sweep of his arm to consult the watch on his wrist. The little hand scurried on and on; it had been scurrying all day. The same question kept coming back to him, carving out a furrow in his mind, and now he just had to ask it.

'Are you going to be dead one day?'

'No,' replied Mister Babbit, 'not necessarily.'